Scream Queen

Scream Queen

stories

Jeremy Griffin

Black Lawrence Press

Black Lawrence Press

Executive Editor: Diane Goettel
Book Cover and Interior Design: Zoe Norvell
Cover Art: "Radha Shooting II (29 Palms, CA)?" by Stefanie Schneider

ISBN: 978-1-62557-152-6

Published 2024 by Black Lawrence Press.
Printed in the United States.

Table of Contents

Stories in this collection have appeared in
the following publications:

“Crimes Like These” in *Beloit Fiction Journal*

“Elliptical” in *BULL: Men’s Fiction*

“The Guidebook to the Evaluation of Revelatory Phenomena” in *Oxford American*

“Inverse Functions” in *Bat City Review*

“Landfall” in *New Ohio Review*

“Raise Your Fists” in *Hopkins Review*

“Reunion” in *december*

“Scream Queen” in *Southern Indiana Review*

“Solve” in *Phoebe*

“Where Strays Might Find Comfort” in *Water-Stone Review*

For Alex, even though there are no pictures.

Crimes Like These

At eight-thirty the gates open and the visitors are ushered in through the metal detectors. After a pat-down from a beefy guard with Skoal breath, it's on to the sign-in desk and then into the commons where they sink down at the tables bolted to the concrete floor and wait for their husbands and sons and brothers and boyfriends to be escorted in from the dorms. Noreen has been making the weekly three-hour trek from Richmond to New River Correctional Unit for six months now, and in spite of herself she's started to take a dark sort of comfort in the process: while the rest of the world collapses around her, it's good to know there are a few things that don't change.

Minutes later, she watches the troop of inmates, clad in hunter green scrubs, shuffle into the room single file. She spots Brandon near the back of the line. As with every other visit, he appears to have aged another ten years, his face a concourse of weary shadows. His chestnut-colored hair hangs in greasy tongues around his fleshy face, which Noreen can see as he moves closer is dappled with fat pink pimples. As a teenager he had terrible acne, thick crusts of it on his face and his back like a rash. It took a 200-mg dose of doxycycline to finally get it under control. Not that it mattered all that much to him; Brandon was never a girl-chaser, never cared about his looks or his social standing the way his classmates did. He was a sullen young man with no use for the world outside of his bedroom, which stayed dark most of the time. Except for the sickly glow of his computer screen.

Noreen swallows him in a hug, one of two they are permitted during her half-hour visit. He smells like cheap soap and sour milk. "What happened here?" she says, indicating the lumpy yellow bruise under his left eye.

"Don't worry about it," he grunts.

"You've lost more weight. Are you eating okay?"

"It's prison, Mom. Not a buffet."

She glances around the busy cinderblock room, the weepy family members and their hollow-eyed criminals. At the table next to theirs, a man with tribal tattoos on his shaved head is arguing with a younger woman in cutoffs and enough eyeliner to paint a mural, their voices hushed but severe. Noreen doesn't even realize she's staring at the man until his eyes fall on hers and she is stunned by the hardness in them, a cool insensibility that makes her look away, chastened.

"Have you talked to Donna?" she asks Brandon.

He nods, picking at a whitehead on his chin. "Says she's gotten the appeal rolling, but it could be months before the judge moves on it."

"Months? Jesus. Did she say anything about moving you out of gen pop?"

"She's working on it. If she can prove there's imminent danger, they're more likely to move me."

"What's there to prove? Did you show her your scar?" His first week in, a group of men targeted Brandon in the bathroom. They fractured his orbital socket and two ribs and one of them sliced his cheek with a razorblade. He got six stitches but refused to say who was behind the attack. A wise move on his part, Noreen has to admit, even despite her desire for justice. But, as he constantly reminds her, hoping for justice does nothing to change the fact that in here he's at the bottom of the food chain, a constant target. The scar, which extends from his eye down his cheek like a tear track, has healed well, but it's a scar all the same, just one more terrible thing he'll have to explain to people once his ten years in here are up.

"Of course I showed her," he snipes. "Damn thing's impossible to miss. But she says it's not enough. She has to prove there's a *pattern* of abuse."

"So then how many times do you have to get beat to shit before she does anything?"

"Lower your voice, will you?" Fearfully, he peers about the commons. The last thing he needs is for the other prisoners to hear him griping to his mother. "All I know is what Donna told me. Until then, I'm stuck in here with everybody else."

•

At home it's time to confront the graffiti on the garage door. It appeared yesterday, the word PERVERT in five-foot-tall black spray paint. Having used the last of the paint thinner on the red circle with a slash through it that someone sprayed on the front door last month, Noreen calls Clayton to borrow some. Twenty minutes later his Silverado sputters into the driveway and out he climbs, all two hundred fifty pounds of him, lumbering across the yard with the metal container in one thick paw. He moves the way you'd imagine a gladiator would entering an arena, slow but with brute purpose.

"Who do you think did it?" he asks as they get started scrubbing away at the paint.

"Some stupid kid probably. It doesn't matter."

"You call the cops?"

"No point." In the past two months alone there have been three flaming bags of dog shit left on the front step, a rock hurled through the picture window, and the circle on the door. Noreen has given a statement to the cops each time, but what can they do? They've got killers and rapists to chase, they aren't going to waste time tracking down petty vandals. Anyway, it could be worse: in the online support groups she frequents they tell horror stories of midnight break-ins, arson attempts, folks having their break lines cut. Retaliation for crimes others close to them have committed. Maybe a little vandalism isn't too high a price to pay for Brandon's wrongdoings

An hour later they've managed to scrub away half the word. They take a break and sit down on the front steps of the modest bungalow, smoking Clayton's Winstons. He slurps one of the beers Noreen keeps on hand for him, while she nurses a lukewarm Diet Coke. Neither of them speaks for a while, which is fine with her; after her visit with Brandon, making small talk is the last thing she wants. The idea of him being relocated to the sex offenders' dorm is both comforting and revolting. Would he be safer there, away from the violent thugs who torment him daily? Yes, but is he any more likely to be rehabilitated? Or would being lumped in with those men, those *animals*, only give him more insights into the trade?

A shaggy-haired kid on a BMX bike cruises past, eyeballing Noreen and Clayton like a pair of dangerous animals. She lifts a hand in greeting, knowing it won't be returned. No one in the neighborhood waves to her anymore. They either ignore her or turn the other way or, occasionally, give her the finger, like the kid does now before speeding off down the road. He keeps his hand upraised until he's out of sight, and right on cue Clayton starts in about Noreen finding a new place to live, one where no one knows who she is.

"Will you at least think about it?" he says, maybe the hundredth time he's asked. "Please?"

Noreen gulps down a mouthful of soda. "Thought about it. Not doing it."

"Why not?"

"I did stuff like that when I was a kid. We egged houses, we fucked with the neighbors. It's just kids being shitty kids."

"And you're fine with that?"

"I'm not letting them run me off like that, Clayton. They'll get bored soon enough and leave me alone."

He sighs a jet of smoke. "And what if they don't?"

"Jesus, what's with all the questions?" She flicks her half-smoked cigarette out into the street. "You're like a toddler. 'Why this? Why that?'"

Clayton looks at the ground between his feet. "Just concerned, is all."

"Be concerned all you want. Just quit with the interrogation."

He finishes his cigarette in silence and drops the butt in the empty beer can and plods back over to the garage door, and of course Noreen feels like an asshole. He's just worried about her, she gets this. But over the past six months she's grown wary of peoples' concern. Too often it's nothing more than a way of masking their judgment. Except that Clayton might be the only person left in her life she can trust not to judge her. He was her first husband, a couple years before Brandon's father, who now runs a spiritual retreat in Utah and hasn't had anything to do with his son since he was three. If she had met Clayton a few years later instead of marrying him right out of high school, things might have worked out. But as it was, they were just going through the same motions their parents had gone through. (Noreen's mother has been married four times; Clayton's father is on his third wife.) And so, when the whole thing fell apart after five years, neither of them was especially surprised. Turns out they got along much better when they had separate houses to go to at the end of the day. It was like leaving a job you had outgrown while remaining cordial with your boss—resentment just seemed like a waste of energy.

•

The next day is Sunday, which means it's her day in the contemporary gallery. Her day to keep tabs on all the flannel-clad hipsters showily pondering the bizarre alien sculptures and the canvases that look like something a sugar-crazed kid might dash off, the Rothkos and the Klimts and the Pollocks. Noreen hates the contemporary gallery, it makes her feel stupid, unsophisticated. She's always believed that art is supposed to offer some sort of escape, like the blotchy pastel landscapes in the Impressionist gallery upstairs. Here, though, the work only compounds the sense she's had for a while that her sanity is being tested.

Still, she knows she's lucky to have a job at all. Working at the Richmond Museum of Fine Arts isn't so bad if you can handle being on your feet most of the day and if you can get past the starchy blue blazer and clip-on tie, and you can't argue with state health and dental. More importantly, even after Brandon's arrest made the local news and most of the papers, the museum was gracious enough to keep her on. She suspects it was simply because they didn't want to pay for the state-mandated security training for a new hire, but at fifty-seven—too old to be shopping around her resume—she's grateful all the same, even if some of the other guards regard her as if she's carrying a lethally contagious disease.

It's 10 AM, which means that the gallery won't be bustling for another hour when the churches let out. While it's still quiet Noreen sneaks away to the main lobby where the monks are working on their mandala. They've been here for the past two days, part of the museum's cultural outreach program. A sign nearby says they're from the Drepung Gomang monastery in Tibet—four workers seated around the four-by-four wooden platform, all in loose-fitting yellow and burgundy robes, their faces obscured by dust masks, and a fifth older one who ambles behind them barking occasional instructions. The four younger men sit cross-legged, bent over at ninety-degree angles. Must be hell on their backs, but if they're in any discomfort they've learned to hide it. The design looks like something you might see in a stained-glass window, an intricate geometric pattern which, using thin hollow styluses, the monks trace with delicate lines of colored sand.

Noreen stands amidst the rest of the onlookers behind the velvet rope surrounding the men, watching them work. There's something peaceful about the scene. Part of it is the ambient droning of chant music coming from a nearby stereo, but mostly it's the painstaking nature of the mandala's construction, the men's collective focus honed to a sharp point. The project, with its charming mosaic character and vaguely cruciform shape, resembles something a group of children might complete in an arts and crafts class, and in fact Noreen is reminded of the week-long art camps she used to send Brandon to in the summertime. Sure, it was cheaper than daycare, but more than that she nursed a lofty hope that maybe it would stoke something in him, a passion, something to motivate him. He'd come home at the end of each day with papier-mâché masks and watercolor portraits and hand-painted mugs and pipe cleaner sculptures, all of which she would display prominently in the kitchen like trophies.

One afternoon when he was thirteen, around the time that his interest in the camps had begun to wane, a volunteer instructor at the camp asked to speak privately with Noreen when she came to pick him up. She'd noticed some disturbing behaviors—Brandon seemed unusually preoccupied with some of the younger girls at the camp, always joking with them, finding reasons to touch them, particularly one girl, an eight-year-old he'd convinced to let him draw her that morning in a closed-off stairwell. The volunteer had found them seated next to each other on the steps, the girl staring forward unflinchingly while

Brandon sketched her profile on a sheet of newsprint, as though this were perfectly normal, just another part of the camp curriculum.

"Don't get me wrong," the volunteer said. She was college-aged, in paint-spattered overalls and pink shoes. "We encourage the students to get to know each other. We want them to form friendships. But Brandon needs to understand what is appropriate and what isn't."

Noreen nodded, pretending to think this over. Really, she was trying to find some way to explain it away. Lately she had been feeling less and less like she knew her son at all. He'd become closed-off and moody, slumping around the house unshowered like a listless specter. This incident only furthered her worry that he was morphing into someone unrecognizable, a stranger in her home.

All the same, he was her kid, and she couldn't help feeling a stab of defensiveness. "But nothing happened, right?" she said. "He was just drawing her?"

The girl pinched her mouth into a line and cleared her throat. "That's what I observed, yes. But the camp directors still find it troubling that he was alone with her at all."

"Look, Brandon's just shy, okay? He has a hard time making friends. I'm sure he was just trying to reach out."

"Maybe you're right," the girl said in the mollifying tone of someone trying to pacify a fussy child. She futzed with her blonde ponytail. "But still, I'm thinking that maybe art camp isn't what he needs right now, Ms. Muntz."

•

Later at home, Noreen logs onto the Mothers of Prisoners Community forum, where she often turns for refuge. She scans the lists of threads, desperate women seeking the advice of strangers. A user with the name Jazzy136, a nurse, says her daughter is going away for six years for aggravated assault, and she's worried she might resort to swiping Percocets from the hospital pharmacy again. HopeFaithJoy wants to know if the disappointment she feels for her son, who's doing a ten-year stretch for armed robbery, makes her a bad mother. *Of course not,* LisaJones6789 replies. *They have to make their own mistakes. We can't protect them from themselves. It doesn't make us bad parents.*

Perhaps not, but Noreen wonders how these women would respond if she told them why her son is locked up. She hasn't had the guts to do so yet. Not just because she's afraid of being shunned from the forums, but also because she's afraid of what it might suggest about her.

She prowls around the house for a while, listening to its familiar creaks and ticks, the sounds of settling like the groaning of old bones. She straightens up the sofa pillows in the living room, unloads the dishwasher, anything to keep herself occupied. Too much free time is dangerous. She's always believed this; the mind starts to turn on itself. Loneliness was a lot easier to manage when she had Brandon living with her. He'd moved in after a conglomerate had bought up his apartment complex and promptly jacked up the rent. Noreen wasn't crazy about the arrangement, sharing a house with her thirty-three-year-old son, but what else could she do? An assistant manager at Red Robin, he barely brought home enough money for gas to get him to and from work—leaving him to fend for himself just seemed cruel. However, having another presence in the house turned out to be more comforting than she'd thought. Did it bother her that Brandon spent most of his free time splayed out in front of the TV in his boxer shorts, or locked away in his room for hours at a time? Was she troubled by his apparent lack of ambition, his absence of friends, or his questionable hygiene? Yes, of course she was—but at least they were together.

In Brandon's doorway she pauses, surveying the empty bed and the bare desk. The police snatched his computer in the raid, as well as her laptop and the modem. All three, she suspects, are boxed up in an evidence locker somewhere. Carefully, as if creeping onto sacred ground, she moves into the room, examining herself in the full-length mirror on the closet door. That she's managed to maintain her slim figure over the years is a blessing, but her age has begun to show in the dark pockets beneath her eyes and the creases around her mouth. Climbing atop the bare bed, she lies on her back with her hands at her chest, vampire style, and she gazes at the popcorn ceiling. She thinks about the raid, the fleet of police cruisers that descended upon the house, the neighbors watching from front porches as a pair of stony-faced officers led Brandon, dressed in sweatpants and a filthy Nationals t-shirt, out to one of the cruisers. As she would later find out, he was one of many targets in a statewide sting operation under the auspices of the state attorney general. She remembers the plainclothes officer who, in the forlorn tone of a doctor delivering bad news, spoke to her while the battalion of uniformed cops tore the house apart. *Pictures*, he explained, *thousands of them. The kind that could land your son in prison for a very long time, Ms. Muntz.* From what their forensic techs could determine, Brandon had been at it for a couple years, downloading and trading them within the kind of depraved online networks you hear about on police procedurals.

Noreen understood the words the man was speaking but had no idea how to process them. They were like puzzle pieces that, in her dazedly sickened state, she couldn't figure out how to put together: surely there had been some sort of mistake, this couldn't be *her* son they were talking about, the same boy who used to sing along to *Sesame Street*, the one who had never even gotten so much as a speeding ticket? The good, sweet, kind-hearted son she had raised on her own?

And yet, didn't it make a twisted sort of sense?

Possibly. Brandon had always been secretive, clamming up whenever she was around, as though he had something to hide. It had occurred to her that he might be depressed, except he wasn't *unhappy* per se, just—*flat*, avoiding human contact whenever possible. If he'd had any interest in a relationship, friendly or romantic or otherwise, Noreen was unaware of it. In fact, he didn't seem to *want* anything, and that bothered her in ways that she had never been able to articulate.

In any case, that's where things start to get hazy. She's told that the same plainclothes officer, seeing that she was in no condition to drive, took her to the station, where Brandon was being held without bond, to give a statement. She's told that upon leaving the station she vomited all over the man's shoes. And she's told that back at the house, which was still being picked apart by forensics technicians late into the night, she had to be sedated with a Xanax. But she can't recall any of this. What she can recall is waking up on the sofa the following morning with Clayton at her side, patting her forehead with a damp washcloth.

"You're okay," he murmured. "Everything's going to be just fine."

•

The next afternoon Brandon calls collect. In addition to his weekly visitation privileges, he gets an hour of phone time a week with good behavior.

"You've got to get a hold of Donna, Mom," he pleads. "They're going to kill me in here, I know it."

"Can't the warden do something?"

"Yeah, right. Dude would just as soon see me dismembered."

Noreen, sitting on the front step steadily working her way through a pack of Dorals, watches a squirrel scamper across the yard. It pauses to look at her and then dashes toward the lone live oak. She glances toward the garage to her right, the bleary shape of the letters still visible even after she and Clayton managed to scrub away as much of the paint as possible. She's probably going to have to repaint the entire door. If only she were like the monks at the museum, stoic, unflappable, at peace with herself and the world, then this might not bother her so much. But she's not like them, not by a long shot. Whatever reservoir of assuredness those men have, hers went dry long ago.

"You think she'll even listen to me?" Noreen asks.

"I don't know, but you have to try. I'm not going to last in here."

"I'll try. In the meantime, just hang tight, okay honey?"

Icily, Brandon replies, "Hey, there's a thought."

•

Wednesday must be a city-wide field trip day because the museum is filled to capacity with students. Harried-looking docents lead them in loose lines from one exhibit to the next, the kids fumbling with their phones, appearing as though they'd rather be anyplace else, and Noreen wishes they were. Aside from her own, she's never liked children, never understood why anyone would. Some people revel in the notion of being responsible for another life, but for her it's never been anything short of terrifying. Brandon was a fluke, a *happy accident* as her mother would glibly tell her friends at church, and as a single mom Noreen spent most of his childhood plagued by unshakable fears: *What if he gets sick? What if he hurts himself? What if he hurts someone else?* That's not to say that motherhood didn't have its rewards. Of course it did; she loves her son more than she would have thought possible. But love can be taxing. It's why she and Clayton couldn't stay married, regardless of how they felt about each other, and it's why she's always secretly been glad she stopped at one child.

Today she's stationed in the main hall. She strolls around the vibrantly colored mandala, surveying it from different angles as though she expects to notice something new amidst the intricacies of its lines. Something she hasn't seen yet. In the center of the design is the image of a seated figure, his legs folded on top of one another, a sprig of flowers in one outstretched hand. According to a nearby placard, this is Bhaisajyaguru, the Medicine Buddha, a great healer of many Eastern faiths. The figure watches her with the dispassionate gaze of a jungle cat stalking its prey. History is full of mystic healers like this one, holy men capable of dispelling illness with nothing more than prayer. Makes you wonder where they all went. You don't hear any more about spiritual nomads obliterating disease with the efficiency of exterminators. Just look at Jesus—cured Peter's mother-in-law and the man in Capernaum and then gave up healing people all together. If Noreen's childhood pastor was to be believed, this was so he could focus on preaching. Only, why did it have to be one or the other, healing or proselytizing? The best she can figure is that maybe Jesus just didn't feel like people deserved to healed anymore. Maybe he thought that some people really were better off gone.

Her reverie is broken when something catches her eye on the far side of the roped-off square, a head of unruly blond hair moving through the crowd. It's the kid from the other night, the one who gave her and Clayton the finger.

Elbowing her way past a gaggle of chittering girls, Noreen circles around behind him, being careful not to be noticed amidst the bustling crowd. Through the forest of heads, she observes him snap off a few selfies with the mandala in the background, each one accompanied by a blast of light from his phone.

She sidles up directly in front of him, but the kid is too engrossed with his phone to notice.

"No flash photography."

He looks up, and with cruel satisfaction Noreen watches as his face goes blank, his mouth falling open, revealing a cumbersome set of braces.

She adds, "It can damage the paintings."

"Other people are doing it," he replies, summoning a gust of bravado.

"I'm not talking to them. I'm talking to you."

He pauses. "I know who you are."

"Good for you."

"You're the pedophile's mom." His mouth twitches in a sinister smirk.

Noreen gnaws the inside of her cheek. Briefly, she considers back-handing him across the mouth. Through grit teeth, she says, "Turn off the flash or I'll have to ask you to leave."

For a long moment, she holds his gaze, the kid's eyes half obscured by the fringe of his hair. It's true that other folks around them are using the flash on their cameras; Noreen has spent most of her day giving this same directive to gawking adolescents. But she's thinking about the graffiti on the garage door, the silhouette of the letters still visible, PERVERT, right there for everyone to see, and the broken window and the bags of dog shit and the slash through the door. Retribution for crimes she didn't commit. Whether the kid is responsible for any of it she doesn't know—he's hardly the only person in the neighborhood with a grudge against her—but it doesn't matter: everyone deserves to be held accountable for something.

But before she has a chance to say anything else, he lifts his phone up to her face and says, "Say cheese!" The flash is blinding, and by the time Noreen has finished rubbing her eyes he has disappeared into the crowd.

•

"Donna, there has to be something you can do," Noreen pleads into the phone. It's taken two days and half a dozen huffy voicemail messages to finally get ahold of Brandon's lawyer.

"I'm doing everything I can, I promise."

"Can't you move things along? He thinks they're going to kill him."

"I wish I could," the attorney responds in a tone of practiced sympathy. "But the appellate courts are so backed up as it is. And, if I'm being honest, Noreen, they tend to drag their feet with crimes like these."

Crimes like these. It's one of those moments in which Noreen can't help wondering if she continues to support her son because she believes deep down he's worth it, or simply because no one else will.

"I'm going to file for a change of venue," Donna explains. "No way was he ever going to get a fair trial in this county after having his image plastered all over the news."

"How long will that take?"

The attorney sighs. Noreen can picture her in her glassy downtown office, her Louboutins stacked luxuriously on the industrial style desk. She's lanky and beautiful in the way of the childfree—Noreen imagines her life as a florid miasma of yoga classes and beach vacations and dinners at restaurants with unpronounceable names. For these reasons she can't help hating her just a little. "Depends. Sometimes months, sometimes longer. It's all up to the judge."

"Christ, Donna. What if it was your kid begging for help, what would you do?"

"I don't have any kids, Noreen."

•

Because after-hours events at the museum pay time and a half, Noreen has volunteered to work the Friday night soiree to celebrate the completion of the mandala. Masses of wealthy patrons stand around the main hall in starchy suits and shimmery cocktail dresses nibbling hors d'oeuvres and clutching champagne flutes like awards. The walls are covered in sixteenth- and seventeenth-century neoclassic tapestries, Flemish and German and French, most of them depicting scenes from the bible. Stationed around the room are sculptures of angels and Greek gods mounted on marble pedestals. And in the center of it all, the finished mandala, the colors as vibrant and sundry as candy, the monks standing by to chat with the guests. Without their dust masks on it's easy to see how young the four workers are, probably late twenties, which makes the older monk, the one in charge, seem ancient by comparison, his face mapped with lines like a dried-up riverbed.

An hour so into the event, everyone turns their attention to the lectern at the front of the room, from which the curator of Asian arts, a paunchy, droopy-eyed man with a bowtie the color of dried blood, now addresses the room: "The sand mandala is more than just a pretty picture," he proclaims with the gravitas of a priest delivering a homily. "It is a meditation on our own impermanence. But this is not a fact to lament. Rather, it is a cause for celebration. For, as the Buddha himself said, when one recognizes the impermanence of all things, one turns away from suffering."

Noreen, standing near the back of the room, watches the fifty or so guests' well-coiffed heads nod knowingly, as if they knew all along he was going to say this.

The man continues, "This is why the mandala will now be ritually destroyed, as a symbol of the temporality of existence, and the sand given to the James River."

The room falls deathly silent as the younger monks assume their positions on all four sides of the platform while the older one, kneeling down at one corner, murmurs a prayer and then, with all the flourish of a magician pulling a rabbit from a hat, produces a horsehair brush from a wooden box nearby. In a move that sends a twinge of bewilderment through Noreen, as though she's witnessing something illicit, he sweeps it through the center of the mandala, obliterating the Medicine Buddha. A week's worth of work, gone with a single balletic stroke. The man makes several more passes with the brush, swirling the colors around, mixing the carmines and corals and azures and blondes and jades, until the entire mandala is just a mass of sand the same wan shade as a cadaver, and all Noreen can wonder is why every beautiful thing in her life has to be wiped away, expunged as if it never existed.

After he sweeps it all into a large silver urn presented to him by one of the younger men, the guests return to their mingling, and Noreen patrols the perimeter of the large room, keeping an eye on the now empty platform. Where the mandala was there is now just a thin skin of leftover sand. What a waste, she thinks. Who needs such a melodramatic reminder that all things are bound to come to an end? If everything is destined to be destroyed anyway, then hastening the process seems foolish and a little cold-blooded.

Eventually the party begins to die down, couples stumbling out to the coatroom, their boozy laughter resounding throughout the halls as they make their way toward the exits. The catering staff begins breaking down the foldable tables and hauling the chaffers down to the café kitchen and gathering up the stray dishes. While everyone is preoccupied, Noreen sidles over to the platform. Glancing up toward the camera in the top corner of the room, she angles her body so that the guard in the security office won't catch her on the monitors swiping a highball glass from a cluttered cocktail table and then ducking beneath the rope surrounding the platform. Sweeping the remaining sand into it with her hand, she tucks the glass inside her blazer and quickly comes to her feet. She casts a look around, but everyone is busy cleaning up after the partygoers.

Everyone, that is, except the older monk, who is studying the statue of Mercury holding a pan flute. When their eyes meet, he gives her a cagey grin like a couple of strangers sharing a moment of levity. Noreen waits for the man to acknowledge her theft, but instead he offers a small bow and then clasps his hands behind his back and shuffles out toward the main lobby, leisurely surveying the works of art along the way. She watches him go, his thick robe skimming the marble floor, his sandaled footfalls barely audible over the clanging noises of the catering staff working behind her.

•

By the time Noreen and Clayton finish painting the garage door on Saturday, it's nearly dark and their ratty clothes are spattered with white droplets. Clayton has agreed to help paint it in exchange for a case of Heineken. Noreen, feeling guilty for prevailing upon him twice in one week, even though she knows he doesn't have any other plans—most of his nights are spent loafing in his recliner after a long day of working at the Meineke in Mechanicsville—insists on making him dinner as well, an offer that he never refuses. As they eat—pan-seared chicken and new potatoes—chattering about their jobs and about old friends from high school, Noreen is transported back to when they first started seeing each other as kids, how they would spend entire nights cruising around the Virginia backroads in his father's truck, talking about the things that seem important when you're seventeen and going sixty on a deserted highway at 1 AM, your heart hammering in your ribs because you're young enough to believe that the world will have at least a little something to offer you. Were they naïve or just stupid? At what point does innocence become a liability?

Soon the conversation winds its way to Brandon, as it inevitably does, and Noreen feels the pall that comes over her any time the subject of her son arises.

“It’s my fault,” she mumbles into her water glass after relating her discussion with Donna. “The whole thing.”

“Come on, no it’s not,” Clayton assures her.

“I must have done something to make him who he is. That’s why he’s there.”

“No offense, Reenie, but he’s there because he’s screwed up, end of story. He’s got his own set of problems. That’s got nothing to do with you.”

Noreen wants to believe him, she does—but privately she’s always wondered if she’s complicit in Brandon’s crimes, just by virtue of being his mother. How much responsibility should she bear for who he is? *Our children are adults*, they might say in the Mothers of Prisoners forum. *We can’t blame ourselves for their mistakes*. On a rational level she understands this. But motherhood isn’t always a domain of rationality. More often than not, it’s a matter of gut instinct, and her gut tells her that she must have failed her son, somehow.

At the corner of the table, amidst all the clutter she pushed out of the way for their dinner plates, sits the glass of sand like a failed botany experiment. When was the last time Noreen applied herself as steadfastly to anything as those men applied themselves to the mandala’s construction? She can’t say. All she knows is that in her mind it had come to represent some larger truth about her own life, something obvious and yet almost impossible to put her finger on. And now the whole thing is gone. She traces the rim of the glass with her fingertip, remembering what the curator said: *When one recognizes the impermanence of all things, one turns away from suffering.*

After a few moments, Clayton takes her other hand in his. His fingers are as thick and stiff as bratwursts.

“It’ll be okay,” he says, a lie, but Noreen is grateful for it all the same. More and more, she’s beginning to think that the truth isn’t worth the pain it causes. She recalls the morning after Brandon’s arrest when, still woozy with Xanax and adrenaline, she awoke to find Clayton hovering over her, caring for her, and she remembers how he told her that everything would be okay, not because he believed it, but because it was what she needed to hear.

That's when they hear the thud against the front of the house.

Slipping her hand from beneath his, Noreen goes into the living room and peers through the curtains. In the middle of the street, straddling his bicycle, is the kid from the museum. He's cradling something in one arm—a carton of eggs she sees as she strains to focus through the dark. He plucks one and chucks it at the house. It explodes against the newly replaced front window in a spatter of runny yellow goop.

Before she understands what she's doing, she is charging for the front door. Later, she will wonder what compelled her to grab the highball glass in the process, but she won't be able to come up with an answer that doesn't feel like a bad excuse. Flying down the front step with the glass in her hand, the hem of her paint-spattered shirt fluttering behind her like a flag, she darts across the yard toward the kid, who, caught off-guard, fumbles with the carton before finally dropping the whole thing on the asphalt and then attempting to flee. However, his hesitation gives Noreen just enough time to catch up to him and grab the back of his t-shirt, yanking him off the bike. He thwacks his head on the ground, which stuns him into immobility, allowing her to climb on top of him, pinning his arms beneath her knees. Squeezing his mouth open with one hand, she brings the glass to his lips. He coughs and sputters and gags like he's drowning as she forces the sand down his throat, but Noreen doesn't relent. Let him feel it, that suffocating panic. Let him writhe and buck and struggle beneath the weight of an immobilizing force. This is what she's wanted for so long, she realizes, not just for the torment to stop but to foist it onto someone else.

Once the glass is empty she clamps his mouth shut with the heel of her hand, the kid now blubbering like a small child, and as it's dawning on her that he might *actually* suffocate, she feels Clayton's meaty hands clamp onto her shoulders and jerk her backward. The glass falls from her grasp, shattering in the tar-streaked road, as he wrenches her off the boy, who, once free, scrambles to his hands and knees and begins hacking up wet gobs of sand. Clambering for his bike, he speeds off down the street, his face snotty and tear-streaked. He casts terrified glances over his shoulder every few seconds as though he expects to see Noreen tearing after him.

"What the hell, Reenie?" Clayton says, his hands still gripping her shoulders. "He's just a kid. What's the matter with you?"

Well, that's the big question, isn't it? The one that keeps her up at night, that haunts her daily, the same one she'll ask herself two weeks from now when the assistant warden at New River Correctional calls to tell her that Brandon is in critical condition after being attacked in the laundry, the assailants having fractured his skull and three of his bones, as well as attempting to castrate him with the lid of a tin can. He'll tell her these things in the offhanded voice of someone ordering fast food, and Noreen will sink down on the kitchen's grimy linoleum floor gasping for air, knowing that she's responsible, that whatever dark authority led to Brandon's crimes surely must have come from her, if only because it answers the question of *why*. It's a shoddy answer but it's an answer all the same, and is there anything more in the world worth wanting?

But that all comes later. All she can think of right now, oddly, is the monk smiling at her, warmly and without judgment, and how good it felt to be *seen*, not as the mother of a monster but as an ordinary person. But you try explaining that to someone like Clayton, someone who's never been viewed as anything other than what he is, and see how far it gets you. And so now, planted on her knees in the middle of the road as if in prayer, the streetlamps stretching out her shadow into something grotesque, Noreen watches the boy disappear around the corner at the end of the road, his sobs echoing back to her from down the street, until once he's out of sight and she begins gathering up the glinting shards of glass, carefully cradling the jagged remains in her bare hands.

Where Strays Might Find Comfort

As far as Esther can tell, the cat lives in the woods on the far side of the manmade pond that runs behind the boxy little houses on Thistle Lane. Not a good place for a small animal, especially considering the recent rumors of an alligator prowling the waters, feasting on turtles and varmints. Probably pushed out of his home by the nearby housing developments going up. The HOA sent out a warning two weeks ago to the entire subdivision advising folks to keep pets and children away from the pond. And so now, after not having seen the cat for over a week, Esther is posting hand drawn flyers on the telephone poles along her street: *Missing: orange tabby. 8-10 lbs. Last seen near the pond. Contact Esther Novitski 349-0525*. She wishes she had a picture of the animal to include, but pictures are for pets, not for mangy strays that come and go as they please. At least this was Vitaly's stance on the matter. To him, cats were not all that dissimilar from mice—pests that tended to linger indefinitely if you showed them even the slightest generosity. He was not entirely wrong. Myrtle Beach is lousy with stray cats living in sewers and under houses, and the city routinely issues warnings against feeding them. Only Americans, he said, with their affinity for unnecessary things, would adopt them as their own.

But Vitaly is gone, leaving Esther alone for the first time in her eighty-three years, and maybe it is because of this that she has come to feel responsible for the animal. And far be it from an old widow to deny herself a little companionship, even if it is with a scroungy stray.

The afternoon is bright and breezy, the dogwoods and crepe myrtles rustling in the tidy front yards. Esther's feet hurt—these days *everything* hurts—but not enough to keep her from shuffling from one telephone to the next, posting the flyers with strips of duct tape in hopes that the coastal winds won't tear them away.

The cat started showing up a few months before Vitaly died, usually in the evenings as the sun was going down and the greasy South Carolina heat had begun to thin. Sometimes Esther would catch her on the back patio snoozing beneath the wicker loveseat or splayed out in a sunny patch of the yard. The cat was a scrawny thing, the knobs of her bones bulging beneath her yellowed skin like a bag of sticks. Her patchy fur was dappled with scabby fleabites. What had drawn her to their home in particular, Esther had no clue, but she could not bring herself to shoo the animal off as Vitaly demanded. She liked the idea that their house was a place where a stray might find comfort.

On the day of the funeral, the cat spent the entire afternoon crouched by the rosebushes in the backyard, spying on the house full of visitors. That evening, when Esther finally had the place to herself, she carried a small slab of *kholodets* on a saucer outside. She set the jellied meat dish at the edge of the patio and then eased herself onto the wicker loveseat. The evening was cool for May, a crisp wind stirring the scrub pines around the pond and casting ripples on the water's glassy surface. A couple minutes later the cat slinked into the glow of the patio light. After an investigative sniff, she began to devour the meal with large, greedy bites. When she was finished, she gave Esther a shy lingering glance as if to offer her thanks and then scampered back off into the darkness.

The next night Esther left a piece of salmon, and the night after that a hunk of lamb from a skewer of *shashlik*, items left over from the funeral reception which she did not have the stomach to finish off herself and that would soon go bad anyway. It was not long before feeding the cat had become a nightly occurrence, something to look forward to. She never attempted to pet the animal, partially for fear of being mauled (the animal seemed friendly enough, though with cats you could never tell), but mainly because she did not want to scare her off. Feeding her was the best way she knew of to show affection.

As Esther is taping a flyer to one of the weather-beaten poles, a security car drifts to a stop in the road behind her. She does not even notice until she hears the guard yell "Hey!" through the rolled down window. "You know you need an HOA permit for that, right?"

Esther turns to face him. Out of spite she has never gotten to know the security officers. This one is dumpy and unshaven, his black Allied Security hat too small for his plump head. *Gus* the patch on his shirt says. Such an ugly name, like a mispronunciation of *gas*.

"For what?" she says.

"The flyers. You can hang them on the bulletin board at the pool, but you need a permit to post them on telephone poles."

"Bah," Esther grunts, flapping a hand at the man before turning back to the pole in front of her. "It hurts nothing."

"Lady, I'm just doing my job here."

"Perhaps you need a different job, yes?"

"You're going to get fined."

"Then let them fine me," she replies over her shoulder. "I have money."

"Don't say I didn't warn you."

Esther spins around to offer a rejoinder—coming from Eastern Europe, she is no stranger to small men overwielding their ounces of power—but the officer is already sputtering away in his little white coupe with the gold star logo on the side.

The security guards were the HOA's well-intended but ultimately misguided response to the plunge in housing prices a couple years ago, which lowered the caliber of families moving into the plan—young broods with no consideration for their neighbors, who blasted music from garages and left their garbage cans out on the curb for too long and sped recklessly through the plan in their monstrous sports cars. The assumption was that the mere presence of uniformed guards would inspire residents to adhere to the HOA guidelines. But the guards are not police, they cannot issue tickets or make arrests or even intervene in the event of a disturbance, like the one Esther overheard between her neighbors last month, the Lupkins, mother and son and, as of late, the mother's boyfriend. A boorish, self-centered lot—well, perhaps not the boy as much as the adults. Esther heard the argument from next door while stepping out back to set out a bowl of *zharkoye* for the cat. The boyfriend, a rat-faced fellow with an adolescent's scanty mustache, was hollering at the top of his lungs at the boy, something about money. Esther could not make out the words, but there was no mistaking the violence in his tone. When she heard a dish smash, she finally called the police. Minutes later she spied through the curtains as the cruiser pulled up to the curb, lights flashing across the houses like a discotheque, and the two broad-shouldered officers marched up to the door, thumbs hooked authoritatively in their belts. The next morning while Esther was watering the hydrangeas out front, she spotted the woman striding out of the house to head off to work, dressed in her bartender's uniform of black slacks and polo. Esther offered her a tentative wave, but the woman regarded her with cold apprehension, as though Esther had stolen something from her, and then climbed in her dented Camaro and jerked out of the driveway.

•

Kyle's shoes are white and blue Nike rip-offs, with arrows on the sides instead of swooshes. Or at least they were that color before he spent the past half hour skulking through the marshy woods, his feet squelching in the mud, sinking up to his ankles in places. Now they're coated in green and gray muck, probably ruined, which was sort of his plan to begin with because maybe now his mom will get him an *actual* pair of Nikes with *actual* swooshes and everybody else will just lay the fuck off him. Especially Todd Barry, who, in homeroom a couple months ago, asked him in front of the whole class if the arrows were there to direct him to guys' anuses, to which Kyle forced a chuckle like he always does whenever Todd rips on him, like he's in on the joke, *haha*, even though it was all he could do not to jab his fingers into the kid's squinty eyes.

So, no, he's not worried about ruining the shoes. Seriously, fuck these shoes. And fuck Todd Barry too, while he's at it.

He's looking for the cat, the one that Ms. Novitsky likes to feed. Thing's been AWOL for a while now, and finding it is the only way he can think of to show his thanks for her calling the cops on Jessie back in July. He'd gone ballistic on Kyle for swiping his credit card and ordering a hundred-dollar pair of Pumas. In Kyle's defense, he had every intention of paying him back eventually, but that didn't keep Jessie from raving at the top of his lungs about respecting other people's property and not being a thieving little fuckwad. Kyle, overcome by a heated gust of bravado, blurted that maybe the whole thing could have been avoided if Jessie had been staying at his own place instead of freeloading at theirs four or five nights a week. The words were out before he could stop himself. That was when Jessie chucked the coffee mug at him. It missed his head by inches, exploding against the kitchen cabinets. He played it off like he had meant to miss, but Kyle got the message all the same. Not long after, the police showed up, and Kyle didn't have to guess to know that Mrs. Novitski, the closest neighbor within earshot, must have called them—a suspicion that was confirmed when, after being led outside with his mom by one of the officers, he caught a glimpse of the old woman peeking through her curtains.

And while Kyle knows he had every right to be pissed at her for sticking her nose into their business, there's no telling what Jessie might have done if she hadn't. So now, having noticed the flyers as he was slumping off the bus, here he is, trudging through the mud and the brambles and the thick-trunked cypress trees with their dripping ribbons of Spanish moss, like a grunt weeding out enemies in some foreign jungle.

Stay frosty out there, Lupkin.

Roger, I'll find the insurgents, sir.

Attaboy. That's why you're the squad leader, because of your bravery and stealth.

Just doing my job, sir.

Your old man would be proud.

Kyle's father was an army staff sergeant who was killed by a sniper while on patrol in Kandahar. Kyle was four at the time, barely able to understand what was happening when the two servicemen and the chaplain showed up at the house one afternoon to break the news. His mother dashed to the bathroom to puke, leaving him alone with the three men, who'd lingered awkwardly in the doorway, their hands clasped in front of them like they were praying, until after a while one of the soldiers held out his fist for Kyle to bump and was like, "How you doing there, little man?" only instead of bumping it Kyle turned and darted down the hall into his room, slamming the door behind him and crawling beneath his bed to wait out the men's visit. He had to clamp his hands over his ears to drown out his mother's bawling, which sounded like the wail of a siren.

But Kyle's not that scared little kid anymore, is he? No sir, and he'll prove it when he enlists after he graduates in five years. Maybe then everyone will stop breaking his balls, Todd and Jessie and all the boys in his P.E. class who call him Bitchtits, as in, *Don't pass the ball to Bitchtits, he'll probably just eat it*, because Kyle is *husky* as his mom calls it. Imagine how they'll all look at him when he shows back up in his dress blues, lean and svelte and handsome, how sorry they'll be about the way they treated him, and Kyle, in an act of boundless grace, will forgive them, because war heroes are supposed to be above grudges.

His leg sinks in a pocket of mud up to his knee. When he yanks his foot free, one of his shoes comes off, trapped in the mud. Shitballs. Briefly, Kyle considers just leaving it there, both shoes, and pressing on barefoot. It would be easier given the marshy terrain, but no: he knows that would only call down his mom's wrath again—Jessie's too. Muddying up the shoes is one thing, but after the whole Puma debacle ditching them altogether seems like a great way to get himself in some deep shit. This time Jessie might not miss with the coffee mug.

It's as he's reaching down to extricate the shoe that he hears movement to his right.

Kyle has just enough time to swivel his head before something thrusts out of the watery scrub—an alligator, he realizes too late, long as a surfboard, its scaly body moving as deftly as a whip, jaws open in a sideways V. Its crooked, nubby teeth clamp around his ankle like a bear trap, and Kyle screams, more out of shock than pain. Staggering backward, he falls on his rear in the mud, struggling to work his foot free, but with each frantic kick the gator twists and flips like a fish, until finally Kyle feels himself being dragged into the brackish water, and, bizarrely, his last thought before being pulled under is that he wishes he hadn't run and hid like a coward when the servicemen came to his house. He wishes he had bumped the guy's fist, taken the news like a goddamn man.

•

Back home, Esther putters around a bit, straightening up the den, unloading the dryer, the television warbling companionably in the background. Keeping herself occupied is important, or so everyone tells her. The trouble is, now that it is just her, there are far fewer chores to be done. She cuts herself a thin slice from the bird's milk cake she made yesterday. In spite of being on her own now, she continues to cook as if for two. Thriftiness does not come naturally when you have spent your entire life shopping for other people. When she goes grocery shopping, she buys far more than she can possibly consume and usually ends up having to throw several items out—either that or feed it to the cat, and despite her voracious appetite the animal can only eat so much.

With her plate of cake, she settles into the recliner to watch the local news. She feels as though she has marched twenty miles and not just to the end of the street and back, although she refuses to use the walker that her daughter Dina got her two years ago after she slipped outside the ValuMart. *You're not a kid anymore, Mom,* the girl had argued. *You have to take care of yourself.* But Esther knows it is a slippery slope from the walker to a wheelchair to just lying in bed all day, a helpless invalid. Dina might as well have presented Esther with a casket.

Strange to think there was a time when she and Vitaly could stroll around the neighborhood for hours before feeling the least bit fatigued, marveling at the immaculate comfort of the suburbs. Esther grew up with her two sisters in the Bednost Tenement in central Brahin, Belarus, a drafty, mold-ridden housing project less than thirty miles from the Polesky Radiological Preserve, part of the Chernobyl exclusion zone. Vitaly, along with his brother and sister, was raised in a dilapidated hovel on the outskirts of town, the children of a fiery-tempered technician at one of the Soviet-era oil refineries. For most of Vitaly's childhood the siblings shared a room, Vitaly sleeping on an old army cot in the closet. Esther and he came to the States in the early nineties after the fall of the Soviet Union, when Lukashenko rose to power and wages plummeted, and beatings from the *militsiya* became increasingly common for those who spoke out against the Council of Ministers. Esther has never gotten accustomed to Americans' blasé attitude toward their own prosperity. They seem hardwired to reject contentment.

It is only because they are young, Vitaly used to say. *They have no history to remind them of what is at stake.*

While Esther suspected that he was right, this always seemed too sympathetic. Too tidy. People should know when they are blessed.

•

It's not in Gus's job description to go around removing flyers from telephone poles. But the recession was hard on the private security industry—for a lot of people it was a luxury they decided to forego—and now Allied is so desperate for contracts that they'll bend over backwards to appease the HOA. Meaning that now he gets to slog up and down the street, tearing down the old lady's missing cat posters, his collar and back and armpits dampening in the cloying heat. You'd think someone from corporate would have the balls to stand up to them, tell them *We're not going to do your damn housekeeping.* You'd think there were more important things to worry about.

At least it's a break from his usual routine, cruising aimlessly around the neighborhood in the farty-smelling Allied Security car, getting the stinkeye from bored teenagers, shooing them off the boat-sized Sycamore Acres sign at the entrance to the plan. But then what can you expect when you're a thirty-nine-year-old GED grad with less than a grand in the bank? Folks don't exactly fall over themselves to offer dudes like him jobs. Anyhow, it's better than being back in the Lowe's lumberyard, hauling two-by-fours and tweezering splinters out of his fingertips.

Once he's claimed all the taped-up flyers, he marches toward the Novitski lady's house. Most of the residents he doesn't know, which is perfectly fine with him, but that one's got a reputation. Case in point, their run-in earlier. *Perhaps you need another job then, yes?* Like he's the gestapo or something and not just some guy trying to make a living. He wishes people would get this, that when he harangues them for, say, playing their music too loud or sneaking into the pool after hours or, sure, hanging flyers without a permit, it's just his job to say something. It's not *him* who gives a shit, it's the people who sign his paychecks.

Studying the crude flyers, he can't help but be reminded of the missing person notices Jared Conwell's mother drew up after Jared disappeared when he and Gus were in the fifth grade. Kid went riding his bike one afternoon and didn't come home. Gus, who'd lived a few streets over from Jared, had nightmares for weeks. He wanted to believe that maybe Jared just took off on his own, hit the road, camping in fields under the stars as he explored the world on his terms. A wanderer like in an old country song. But even at ten years old, he understood that wasn't true. People don't just take off like that. Someone disappears like Jared did, you can bet they're not coming back.

Which is exactly what happened. Weeks went by, months, but no Jared. It became common to find the Conwells passing out flyers downtown and knocking on doors and canvassing huge swaths of the low country. You'd go to the mall and there Mrs. Conwell would be, with her frizzed-out hair and sleep-deprived eyes, badgering shoppers with Jared's school photo. People started going out of their way to avoid her.

Now, as Gus mounts the Novitski woman's front steps and lays the stack of sheets on her welcome mat like a cat depositing a dead bird, he tries to expel the memory from his mind. Dwelling on the whole Jared thing is only going to leave him in even more of a funk. The strips of duct tape bind the pages all together in a sloppy bundle, though apparently not well enough because as soon as he turns to walk away a strong breeze comes through and scatters them across the yard, and for Gus it's like *of course*. You can't just do your job and move on—there's always a hitch, always something gumming up the works. If there's a metaphor for his entire life, that's it right there.

Hiking up his sagging pants, he goes trotting after the flyers, his belly jiggling beneath his starchy shirt. They swirl in the air, dancing their way up the street toward the highway. He manages to snag one, but by the time he gets to the cul-de-sac at the end of the street he's already too winded to chase down the rest. As a kid he used to spend entire afternoons zipping around on his bike, sweaty from the heat but not from the exertion. Now a brief trot down the street leaves him bent over with his hands on his knees, struggling to catch his breath, his vision spotty. This is what time does to you, he thinks, it beats you down until you no longer recognize yourself.

With his one sad flyer, he returns to the woman's front step, his face slick with sweat. At this point it's probably not even worth leaving it, but returning them to her was never the point. The point was to send a message: follow the damn rules. Except, if he's being honest with himself, on some level he respects the fact that she blew him off. Sure, it only makes his job harder, but there's something admirable about her refusal to fall in line. He could use a little bit of that himself, some grit. Maybe then he wouldn't be here lumbering around in the hot sun, bemoaning his station in life. Securing the flyer in place with the small gnome sculpture by the door, Gus returns to the Allied car idling at the curb, still thinking about Jared but trying hard not to. Even now, pushing forty, there's a part of him that still cowers at the thought of the kid being snatched off his bike so easily. By now Gus should have outgrown that fear—right?

Instead, he focuses on the Novitski lady, with her stern schoolmarm face, her body squat and troll-like. He wonders how she will react when she comes across the flyer, and he wishes he could be there to see it.

•

It is just after eleven PM when Esther, hobbling into the kitchen for a glass of water, spies the police lights through the front window. Her first thought is that the Lupkins have gotten into another domestic squabble. But when she peers through the curtains she sees the woman and her boyfriend standing in the yard holding each other like a couple of frightened children, the woman taking quick, shaky drags off a cigarette. An officer is talking to them, making notes in a little black notebook.

Clutching the front of her robe closed, Esther slips out onto the front step. If something serious has happened, a burglary perhaps, she deserves to know. The woman spots Esther lingering outside her house and hustles over. "Have you seen him?" she implores. She is short, not much taller than Esther herself, her auburn hair threaded with white streaks.

"Seen who?" Esther says.

"My boy. My son. Kyle. Have you seen him today?"

"I have not."

"Shit," the woman huffs, puffing on her cigarette. She cradles her forehead in her free hand. The swirling crimson lights of the cruiser split her face into a concourse of haggard shadows.

"He is missing?"

"I got home from work and he wasn't there. I figured he was out riding his bike or something. But no one's seen him."

Esther descends the steps. Up close she can see that despite the grooves on her face the woman is quite young, early thirties perhaps. Just a child herself. "I am sure he will be found," she reassures her. Gesturing vaguely in the direction of the swampy forest, she adds, "Perhaps he is lost in the woods, yes?"

The woman shakes her head. "He knows he's not supposed to go in there."

"Yes, but boys. Always doing what they should not be doing, yes?" Esther offers her a smile, but it feels all wrong, phony.

The woman tucks her hair back behind her ears. "Just let me know if you see him, okay?"

"Of course."

She plods back over to the boyfriend. Esther watches her curl into his embrace, the cigarette jutting from her mouth like a single fang.

All of the commotion has left her unable to sleep, and so she ambles into the kitchen for something to eat. On the refrigerator, held up by a Garfield magnet, is the single flyer that someone left on her welcome mat. She should have known the HOA would stoop so low. She will simply have to make more, show them that she will not be bullied. For now, though, she takes the bird's milk cake out of the fridge. The single slice she had earlier reveals the spongy layers of the chocolate-covered pastry. Pouring herself a glass of milk, Esther begins to eat from the cake directly, a faux pas most certainly, but there is no one around to see her. Through the window the lights of the cruisers flash on the walls, and all at once she is thrown back to the day that she found Vitaly in the yard. He had suffered a stroke while pruning the rose bushes. When she came across him, he was lying on his back clutching the wooden-handled shears, his face locked into a look of wide-eyed perplexity, as if he had died in the midst of a startling realization. A cadre of vehicles, police cars and an ambulance and even a firetruck, had swooped in to retrieve the body. Since then, even the distant echo of a siren is enough to make Esther's nerves ring like tuning forks.

Ordinarily the cake, one of Vitaly's favorite treats, would last Esther at least a week. But she is so absorbed in the memory that she almost does not realize she has devoured the entire thing in one sitting, not until she feels a tremor in her gut, and she hobbles to the bathroom just in time to vomit it all up. Sweating and panting, she remains seated on the floor with her back against the bathtub, waiting for the nausea to subside, for her body to feel empty again.

•

Gus is wearing duck boots, and his feet squish up to his ankles in the gray-green muck. The sheriff's deputies have given all twenty of the searchers orange vests and whistles in case they find anything. *Be on the lookout for critters*, one of the deputies told them. *No telling what's living back here.* Gus has heard the rumors of the gator, and he keeps a watchful eye on the pools of water all around him. The last thing he needs is to lose a foot or a leg. Would his health plan even cover that?

Two days and no kid. Not a good sign. If there's one thing that he knows from watching *SVU*, it's this: if you don't find the missing person within forty-eight hours, it's not likely you're ever going to find them. In the meantime, a fleet of news vans has assembled at the entrance to the subdivision like a pack of hungry animals, the pretty business-skirted reporters speaking soberly into tripod-mounted cameras. He spends most of his days making sure they don't hassle the residents, who are understandably shaken.

If there's any silver lining to this whole mess, it's that it's given him plenty of opportunities for OT. That's the only reason he's agreed to join the search crew, because the boss is allowing him to stay on the clock. Well, not the *only* reason—Gus isn't completely heartless, he wants to find the kid as much as anyone. But making a few extra bucks in the meantime certainly sweetens the deal.

The crew creeps through the trees, ducking beneath branches and swatting at the Spanish moss and kicking over piles of leaves and pine needles in search of clues, although Gus's mind isn't really on the search. It's on Jared Conwell. If the missing cat flyers were a reminder of that whole episode, then this is like reliving the entire experience. Some things, they rip a hole in your life that you maybe don't notice at the time but that you're never able to stitch closed again. You look back years later and it's like, right there, *that's* where things started to slip. And that's how it was with Jared's disappearance. After something like that, school just didn't seem worth it anymore to Gus, not when you could just vanish any second without a trace. When his grades bottomed out, his parents tried tutors and counselors, but what was the goddamn point? Nothing made sense anymore. A kid Gus had known, who he'd ridden bikes with more times than he could count, was gone and the world just kept turning and how could anyone not think that was totally fucked up?

Once, a year or two after Jared's disappearance, Gus happened to run into Ms. Conwell at the county fair. She was outside the gated entrance holding a poster board with a picture of her son on it, their phone number printed in large block letters at the bottom. "Gus Meacom!" she cawed when she spotted him, swallowing him up in a bony, musty-smelling hug. "How *are* you?"

"Fine," Gus replied. The friends he'd come with had quickly breezed past the woman and were now lingering inside the entrance behind Ms. Conwell's back, sniggering. Gus, chunky even then, hadn't been quick enough to dodge her.

"You're getting so big!"

"Thanks."

"How's school, sweetie?"

"It's good."

"Yeah? What's your favorite subject?"

Gus glanced around at all the people flooding past them, giving the woman a wide berth. Like maybe she was carrying some kind of deadly disease.

"I have to go meet my friends," he muttered, slipping out of her embrace.

But Mrs. Conwell grabbed his arm as he was moving away. That manic smile remained, but there was something menacing in it now. Something dangerous.

"It could have been you, you know," she said, conversational, as if she were commenting on the weather.

"Ms. Conwell, I have to—"

"It could have easily been you, Gus. You lucky little shit."

Jerking his arm back, Gus broke free from the woman's grasp. He hustled over to his friends. As they ambled to the ticket booth, he threw one last look over his shoulder at Mrs. Conwell, standing alone in the sea of people like a shark in a school of fish.

So now here he is, tramping through the muggy woods in search of another missing kid, and you have to wonder: if Jared had never disappeared, is this still where Gus would have ended up? Or might he actually have done something with his life? Would he even want to know?

But hello, what's this? Something half-submerged in the mud. A shoe, he sees as he tromps closer. Gus glances around. He can just make out the nearest searcher's hunter orange vest about a hundred yards away. Too far for him to call over. Hunkering down, he pulls the thing out of the muck. It makes a sound like something being slurped up a vacuum cleaner. He studies the shoe the way a man might study an unfamiliar hair on his wife's blouse, a mixture of apprehension and disbelief. It's blue and white and caked with gray gunk, the laces still tied.

His first thought is that the kid is probably dead, which means Gus can say bye-bye to anymore overtime. His second thought, though, is that maybe there's an opportunity here. No one ever found a trace of Jared, not a shoe or a hat or body or a damn strand of hair. But this here could be an honest-to-god clue to the missing kid. And *he* found it, him, Gus Meacom, and who knows, maybe this will be the clue that solves the case. He'd be a hero. There'd be newspaper articles, TV interviews. A life-changer.

For some reason, the image of Mrs. Conwell smiling down at him with that twisted grin of hers flashes through his mind.

You lucky little shit.

Gus grabs the whistle around his neck and blows.

•

Ten PM and the air outside is warm and silky with moisture. Rain on its way, no doubt. Esther sits in the patio loveseat listening to the creatures in the woods tweet and caw and croak. Sleep has become a luxury, something she can only wish for. "We glory in our sufferings," says Romans 5:3-4, "because we know that suffering produces perseverance; perseverance, character; and character, hope." Father Kozlov read this verse at Vitaly's funeral, and as much as Esther wanted to take comfort in the sentiment, it felt too patronizing. Why must suffering be the precursor to clarity? Why can an all-powerful god not offer the latter without the former? She felt the same way at the reception, with all of the casserole-bearing well-wishers rattling off their inane benedictions. *God has a plan. Everything happens for a reason.* Esther did not bother pointing out that a reason does not always justify an outcome. Criminals have reasons, killers and rapists, but no one would dare excuse their actions on those grounds. A reason is not a validation, only a motive.

In her hand she holds the flyer from the refrigerator. She is not sure why she felt compelled to take it off the fridge—perhaps out of some childish hope that it would magically prompt the cat's return. In any case, she has yet to tape up any new ones; the news of the missing boy has everyone upset, justifiably so, and posting a new set of flyers seems in poor taste. Besides, they would probably just be torn down again. One would think the HOA would *want* the animal recovered, if only because it might make them appear charitable by association. But if there is one thing that Esther knows about regimes, it is that charity runs counter to their objectives.

A few yards away the Lupkins' back door squeaks open, and Esther watches Ms. Lupkin glide out into the yard and light up a cigarette. She dips her head at the woman in somber recognition. As if having been beckoned, Ms. Lupkin drifts across the grass and sinks down into the plastic Adirondack chair across from the loveseat. Her face is as drawn and color-leeched as an old rag. The polite thing would be to offer her something, a drink perhaps, but Esther knows that nothing she can offer will give the woman what she needs.

"They found a shoe," Ms. Lupkin says, expelling plumes of smoke from her nostrils.

"Yes, I heard this."

"No body, though."

Esther does not say anything.

"Why would he lose his shoe?" the woman asks. "And why just one?"

"Children, they do this. My daughter, she lose things all the time when she is young. She lose her retainer many times. We have to go looking through the trash to find it. Very unpleasant. But that is kids. A shoe, this does not mean anything."

The woman, clearly aware that she is being placated, gives Esther a look. "Where are you from, anyway?" she says.

"Belarus," Esther answers.

"Where's that?"

"In Eastern Europe." Then, because Americans are only able to orient themselves by their proximity to their enemies: "Next to Russia."

"Yeah, I thought you sounded Russian." The woman flicks the butt out into the yard. Esther watches the ember's arc out into the darkness as if observing the trajectory of a missile. She stops herself from asking the woman not to dispose of her cigarette butts in her yard. Then Ms. Lupkin worms her hand into the pocket of her ratty jeans for another one. "My husband's grandmother was Russian, this little round blue-haired lady. Real sweet. Smelled like peppermint and onions."

"They are all little and round and blue-haired," Esther jokes.

"You're not."

"I am not Russian."

"Well, to the folks around here you might as well be, that accent of yours."

"To these folks I am an old widow, that is all."

"We all gotta be something," Mrs. Lupkin says, lighting up. Her voice has the aloof quality of someone talking in her sleep. She gazes out toward the moonlit pond. "I was sorry to hear about your husband."

"Thank you."

"I never got a chance to talk to him, but he seemed like a good guy."

"He was. A very good man."

"My husband died, too," Ms. Lupkin continues, "In Afghanistan."

"When was this?"

"About ten years ago. He got shot by a sniper. Kyle was just a kid."

"This is terrible."

Shrugging, the woman puffs on her cigarette. "You'd think I'd be used to losing people. You'd think I'd be a pro by now."

Esther has to keep herself from reminding the woman that the boy is not lost yet, only missing. She understands that the body can only hold so much—sometimes you have to spill your guts to make room for your grief. It could be that this is why she considers telling her about the day she found Vitaly in the yard, what happened at the hospital. The nurses had given her a few minutes alone with him in a curtained-off med bay. Vitaly lay on his back with the sheet pulled up to his tawny bare chest. Sitting motionless beside him, Esther watched her deceased husband's colorless face as a child might watch a balloon ascending into the sky, her heartbreak and her rage competing for purchase in her gut. To her own dismay, she found herself fuming at him, a cold, visceral anger that she had not experienced in decades. It had heft, this anger, weight. Of course Vitaly's death had not been deliberate, but when you are staring down at your dead husband of over fifty years it is impossible not to feel otherwise.

She slapped him across the face, hard enough to make her palm sting. A small part of her half expected his eyes to pop open. When they did not, she slapped him again, harder this time, and then again, over and over with both hands, pounding against his slack face and his bare chest and his shoulders, her knuckles knocking unceremoniously against his old bones, her breath coming in ragged huffs as she pulled at his hair and clawed at his skin, until Dina and her husband Brian, alerted by the commotion, rushed in and wrestled her away from the bed, Esther's face streaked with tears and snot, her teeth gnashing like an animal caught in a trap.

The woman motions to the flyer in Esther's hand, rousing her from her daze. “I’ve seen that cat prowling around by the pond. You think something’s happened to it?”

“I do not know,” Esther replies. She looks down at the flyer as if she forgot that she was holding it. “I hope not.”

“Maybe someone took her in.”

Esther shrugs. “It is silly, being sad over a cat. This cat is not even mine.”

“You can love something that doesn’t belong to you. It isn’t silly.” The woman hoists her cigarcttc in the air. “Here’s hoping everything turns out okay.” She takes a deep drag.

Esther looks over at the woman, smoking in the dark. Okay for whom? Perhaps it is possible to love something that is not yours, but then how can you know whether it belongs to you in the first place? She glances down at the crumpled flyer. What might she say to know that at this moment Gus Meacom, on the opposite side of town, also unable to sleep, is considering this very notion, that maybe all love amounts to is the devastation you feel when something is taken from you, and how steadfastly those losses can stay with you? How would she react to seeing him, spurred by the curious resolve he has felt since finding the shoe, a sense of courage he has not experienced since he was a child, climb from his bed and sit down at his computer in his boxer shorts to print up new flyers, fancier ones this time, which he will post on telephone poles in the Sycamore Acres development to replace the ones he tore down, the HOA be damned?

Possibly she would be buoyed by this. But Esther does not know these things. All she knows is that she is not ready to give up searching for the cat, to accept loss. And so a moment later she comes to her feet and wanders into the kitchen. She paws through the refrigerator, gathering up cartons of deli meats and Saran-wrapped leftovers, as much as she can hold, and then hauls it outside. She slings cold cuts out into the yard like Frisbees, tosses hunks of pot roast and whole pieces of apricot chicken, the sweet brown glaze leaving her fingers sticky. Then she heads back inside for another armload of food, all of the extraneous items she purchased because she does not yet know how to be alone, and this time the Lupkin woman follows her. She does not say a word to Esther. She does not need to. Together, they tear apart the kitchen for foods that might attract the cat, cans of diced chicken and pouches of tuna, blocks of cheese, a carton of vanilla ice cream, carrying it all outside and tossing it into the grass like an offering to a god, until the yard is strewn with food. Then they collapse back into their seats, gazing out at the delectable mess they have made, and they wait, silently, for the animal to slink into the light.

The Guidebook to the Evaluation of Revelatory Phenomena

1993

At over seven feet tall, including the three-foot base, the statue was big enough that Connelly had to teeter on a wobbly stepladder to examine the eyes, which were bulbous and heavy-lidded, as if the figure was on the verge of sleep. It was a bronze depiction of the Virgin Mary, sculpted around a plaster cast, and if the parishioners of Our Lady of the Nazarene were to be believed, it had been weeping oil for the past two days.

"You haven't seen anybody tampering with it?" Connelly asked Father Ortiz, who was hovering behind him like a giddy child, worrying the tiny wooden cross around his neck.

"Never. Nobody here would do that."

You'd be surprised by what people will do, Connelly almost retorted, but as a priest he was supposed to remain optimistic. He didn't want to come across as cynical, a *drama queen* as Allison would have called him. His late sister, ever the pragmatist. And while it never failed to make Connelly feel chastened, now he would give anything to hear it again, to be teased by his big sister once more.

With his polaroid, he snapped a few pictures of the statue's face, slick with moisture, like water dribbling down a rockface, and then shook the flimsy prints to develop them. With his free hand, he dipped his fingertip into one of the two tracks of liquid and sniffed it. Sweet, florid. "It's scented."

"It's sacramental then, yes?" Father Ortiz asked.

"Can't say yet," Connelly replied, descending the ladder. Palming the sweat off his forehead—like everything else in the church the AC was on the fritz, and the sanctuary was stifling—he stood back to examine the statue in its entirety, the figure's veiled head angled downward in an attitude of serene benevolence, palms together at the clavicle.

"Esto es un milagro," Father Ortiz whispered, bringing the cross to his lips. *It is a miracle.*

Connelly didn't bother to point out that it was far too early to make such a determination. Not to mention that, according to the sixty-page *Guidebook to The Evaluation of Revelatory Phenomena*, disseminated through the Vatican's Office of Pontifical Commissions, the diocese couldn't make such a proclamation—that was up to the Holy See, and it generally took a few hundred years. Besides, in all likelihood there was an earthly explanation: the Church, for all its mystery, was no stranger to hoaxes.

Still, no need to dash the Father's hopes just yet. Or, for that matter, the hopes of the fifty or so congregants lingering outside in the parking lot to see the statue, La Virgen Llorona as they had come to refer to it, to witness proof of the divine. They would find out soon enough that there were no rewards for their faith.

After giving the figure a cursory examination, Connelly and Father

Ortiz retired to the father's office to review the camcorder footage one of the congregants had taken the previous day. The room was little more than a converted supply closet in the back of the chapel, rank with old incense and mold, barely big enough to accommodate the battered metal desk behind which both men now sat. Leaning in close enough to the small grainy TV screen that their heads almost touched, they observed the shaky footage of the liquid streaming down the length of the statue. A chorus of gasps and invocations rose up from the crowd of observers as the oil dampened the cream-colored cloth on which the statue sat.

"Tomorrow we'll take a look at the ceiling, see if there are any leaks," Connelly said.

"We checked. It was patched a couple years ago after Hurricane Andrew."

"I still need to look."

"Yes, of course."

On the screen, the point of view swung away from the statue, out over the roomful of witnesses, some of them praying silently with their eyes shut, others holding their arms aloft in exaltation.

"And I'll need to talk to these folks," Connelly added.

"These are good people." Father Ortiz replied, a thorn of defensiveness in his voice. "They wouldn't have anything to do with this."

"I understand," Connelly said. "This is just protocol. It's required."

With a nod that said he wasn't entirely sold on the idea, the father returned his attention to the screen. What Connelly wanted to say but had once more stopped himself from voicing for fear of invoking his sister's imaginary mockery was, *Everyone has something to hide.*

•

Our Lady of the Nazarene was a boxy brick structure situated on a boggy parcel of land just outside of Ville Platte. The white paint was flecked and peeling, the steeple canted to one side like a party hat. Half of the stained-glass windows were shattered, covered over with waterlogged cardboard. Connelly couldn't help thinking that the hundred or so congregants would have been better off abandoning it, finding a new house of worship, someplace other than this crime-ridden burg of shuttered businesses. But then, as in the case of his own diocese in Shreveport, the local townships had never been exactly welcoming to immigrants, an attitude that he had been trying for some time to rectify through outreach programs, but with little success.

This, anyway, was the archbishop's reasoning for tapping him to investigate the statue, because of his relationship with the Hispanic community. Despite his reservations about languishing in the south Louisiana summer sun for who knew how long, Connelly had accepted the appointment, because if someone was indeed playing a trick on the members of the church, it seemed imperative that he be the one to expose it.

Then again, having never taken part in this sort of inquiry, he had no idea what to look for. He was only thirty-five, practically a child in his profession, vice-chancellor of his diocese for less than a year. It probably would have made more sense for the archbishop to have sent a professor or scientist, someone with critical expertise, but discernment of a purported revelatory event could only be undertaken by someone with "sincerity and habitual docility towards Ecclesiastical Authority"—this according to the *Guidebook*, which Connelly carried in a blue report binder, allowing easy access for note-jotting, and which he had spent the past few days poring over like a student cramming for a test.

Of course, had the archbishop known about Connelly's state of mind ever since Allison's murder the previous fall, he surely would have yanked him right out of Our Lady of the Nazarene, possibly even removed him from his own parish. Which might not have been so terrible, because at least then he wouldn't have had to stand up in front of his congregation week after week blathering about God's benevolence, his feeling of fraudulence only amplified by his unshakable love for the Church. He loved the sense of community, the rich history of tradition. And his parishioners, he loved them too. He dined with them, went bowling with the Youth Group. Even something as dismal as administering last rites had its charms because it made him feel useful, an instrument of good.

Strange, then, to know that if anyone could appreciate the glaze of doubt that had settled over his brain, it would have been Allison, the only other churchgoer in the family. Of his four sisters, Connelly—the youngest, younger than her by two years—had always been closest with her. Because of their parents' hectic work schedules (their father a lawyer, their mother a commercial realtor), and because his other sisters were too old to find him interesting, she had spent much of their younger years looking after him. They played together in the forest at the edge of their neighborhood, scrabbling up the magnolia trees, lazing amidst the thick-leaved branches. On weekends, they would stay up late watching TV together, sprawled on the living room carpet with their feast of Nilla wafers and bottled sodas. Even now, Connelly couldn't see a Coca-Cola ad without recalling those evenings with his sister zoned out in front of *That Girl* and *I Dream of Jeannie*.

Ironically, it was also Allison who had questioned Connelly's motivations when he announced to the family, at twenty-two, his interest in attending seminary. In her view, entering into the priesthood was as weighty a commitment as joining the military. "It isn't a joke, you know," she'd warned him. They were sitting on her back patio, the rest of the family inside. Overhead, gnats swirled in the glow of the porch-light. "You can't just coast."

"I know that. I'm serious about it."

"You've never been serious about anything."

"That's not fair," he protested, though she had a point. He had never been a model student. It was only by the grace of a couple sympathetic professors that he had eked through college the previous spring, at which point he'd realized how much he'd longed for the stability that the Church had brought him when he was young. He'd always liked helping people—as a teenager he'd gone on mission trips and worked with Habitat for Humanity—and he wanted to impart that sense of stability onto others. He added, "People can change, you know."

"Not that much."

"Since when are you such a cynic?"

She batted a mosquito away from her face. "I'm a Christian, but I'm also a realist."

"Come on, Allie. I was really counting on your support."

"I'll support you no matter what," she said in the tender tone one might use to say goodbye to a friend. Only those closest to her knew that her stony veneer was a façade, that beneath it she was warm-hearted almost to a fault. "I know this is a big deal for you. I just need you to understand the kind of commitment you're making."

•

That night, after his daily phone debriefing with the archbishop, in whose voice Connelly could hear the unseemly exhilaration of a man who believed a cardinalship might be in his future, he ordered a BLT from room service. "What brings you to town?" the waitress asked when she delivered the sandwich twenty minutes later.

"I'm doing some work with a local church. I'm a priest."

The woman's face lit up. She paused transferring the dishes from the dining cart to the small table in the corner, where Connelly had been studying the bleary polaroid snapshots, searching for an aperture in the figure, an opening through which to pour the oil. "Wait, are you talking about the statue? The one that's been crying?"

"You heard about that?"

"Saw it in the news. La Virgen Llorona?"

Connelly deflated a little. Evidently, his advice to Father Ortiz to avoid the press had gone unheeded—although maybe it had been naive to think that exposure was avoidable at all. Everybody loved a good scoop, especially one that threatened to embarrass the Church. Nonetheless, this would only make it that much more devastating to the community when the whole thing turned out to be a joke.

"Well, I guess the secret's out," he said.

Stuffing her hands into the pockets of her black slacks, she said, "So, what do you think, is it a sign from God?" With her narrow frame and bun of hickory-colored hair, she reminded him of Allison, a kind of practical beauty. But then, everyone reminded him of his sister these days.

"I have my doubts."

"Why?"

"Because if He really wanted to reveal Himself to us, He should start by addressing suffering, not by dazzling us with parlor tricks. Otherwise, He's not much better than a party magician."

Right away Connelly wished he could cram the words back into his mouth. This wasn't confession, the woman was just being nice. Plus, hadn't he counseled people about this very thing, about not holding God accountable for the ills in their lives? The Lord didn't cause pain without allowing something new to be born, or so claimed Isaiah 66:9. However, now that Connelly had found himself on the receiving end of tragedy, he could think of no better place to direct his anger than the Almighty.

"Sorry," he muttered, removing a wad of bills from his wallet on the dresser, far more than necessary for a tip. "It's been a long day."

"No worries," she responded, tucking the money into her shirt pocket, nodding her thanks. "I'm Episcopalian anyway."

•

On a Tuesday morning the previous September, just before ten o'clock, a man named Gary Iverson strode into the Fort Worth DMV, where he'd been employed until two weeks prior, and sent a spray of semiautomatic gunfire across the lobby. Eleven people were killed, including Allison, who had been there to renew her driver's license. At the burial, during which Connelly had sat paralyzed beside Allison's husband and their three children, the priest—a friend who had volunteered to officiate—had read from Revelations, verse 21:4: "He will wipe every tear from their eyes. There will be no more death or mourning or crying or pain, for the old order of things has passed away." Later that night, Connelly, unable to sleep in his sister's chilly guest bedroom, retrieved his bible from his bag and turned to the passage. Countless times he had recited it for grieving spouses and children and siblings and friends, always enlivened by its hopeful sentiment. Now, though, as he slumped on the edge of the bed in his underwear peering down at the page, the highlighted verses and the notes scribbled in the margins, it seemed to take on a new sort of heft. Something had indeed passed away, of that he was certain. As for what the new order would be, he couldn't say.

Before he was able to stop himself, he'd torn the page out of the book. For a few moments, all he could do was sit there with it in his lap, unsure of what to do next. He'd never defaced a holy object before, and it felt both obscene and thrilling, not unlike his and Allison's clumsy forays into cursing when they were kids. When he was certain there would be no smiting from on high, he folded it up and tucked it into the book. Ripping the page out was one thing, but he could hear Allison cautioning him against disposing of it altogether. To her, that would have seemed too final, a door he could never reopen.

•

Because most of the congregants spoke little English, and because Connelly's Spanish was rudimentary at best, Father Ortiz translated during the witness interviews, which Connelly captured on a handheld recorder. The questions all came directly from the *Guidebook*: Did the interviewee know anyone who might benefit from the potential hoax? How, in their estimation, might such an event might be faked? If real, did they believe the event to be the work of God or Satan? For the most part, the responses were all the same—nobody knew anything, and Connelly had a feeling that even if they did, they wouldn't tell him. Most of them regarded him with the apprehension reserved for law enforcement, and in fact that was precisely how he was beginning to feel, like a cop on some gloomy police procedural, pulling at threads that went nowhere.

"The Lord has revealed Himself to us, why don't you believe it?" one woman said, the church secretary, Anna Lucia Alvarez, who had been seated only feet away from the statue when the phenomena began.

"It's not that I don't believe," Connelly responded. "But I have to be impartial."

"How can you be impartial about God?"

"That's what I'm trying to ascertain, if it really is God's work."

"Look around, Father Connelly." The woman gestured to the small, shabby sanctuary, the rotting pews and the cracks zigging across the concrete floor. She was squat, late seventies probably, her face as coarse as a relief map. "We don't have a lot of money. The Lord knew that if he showed Himself to us, people would come and we'd be rescued. La Virgen Llorona has saved us."

Connelly studied the woman the way a person might study a postmodernist painting, a mixture of admiration and perplexity. She was certainly right about Our Lady of the Nazarene having been rescued from bankruptcy. Whereas the church had barely been treading water a few days ago, now it was drawing in more relief than anyone knew what do with. In the past three days alone, people from all over the country had sent in over forty thousand in cash donations, and the money was still coming, sometimes in the form of cash envelopes deposited at the base of the statue during visiting hours, alongside the trinkets and letters and candles and photos of loved ones that supplicants would leave in hopes of invoking the Virgin's grace. But then, that was the issue, wasn't it? A church on the brink of foreclosure suddenly comes into a fortune—who wouldn't be skeptical?

Later that afternoon, after the interviews, Connelly and Father Ortiz sat quietly in the priest's stuffy office. Through the opened windows, over the clatter of the ancient desk fan, they could hear the clamor of the crowd, which had swelled to the hundreds after the footage of La Virgen Llorona had hit the local news. It had taken him nearly ten minutes that morning to find a parking spot amidst the sea of vehicles spilling into the overgrown fields on either side of the parking lot and then to shoulder his way through the mob to the church doors. Some folks had carried poster signs bearing bible verses; a few others toted giant crosses as if they were auditioning for *The Passion Play*. Camera crews roved throughout, interviewing anyone who would talk, while a handful of shameless vendors hawked bottles of water and cans of soda for outrageous prices.

"Have you thought about what you're going to tell your parishioners when this turns out to be hoax?" Connelly asked the father.

"If."

"Right, *if* it turns out to be a hoax."

The priest leaned back in his seat and laced his fingers across his large belly. He was plump in the jolly way of men who have come to terms with their appetites, his bulging ears tufted with silvery fur. "I'm hoping I won't have to."

"I just worry about getting their hopes up."

"Let them hope." The man touched the cross resting on his broad chest. "These people have very little. For some of them, the church is it. Let them believe that God is speaking to them."

Connelly let this sit between them for a moment. "That doesn't strike you as a little reckless?"

Shrugging, the father smiled like a doting parent to a precocious toddler. "What can I tell you? Faith *is* reckless."

•

Iverson's trial had been predictably short, barely a week. The prosecution assailed the jury with blown-up images of the crime scene, the bodies slumped in molded plastic chairs or splayed out on the scuffed tile floor. Blood spattered the walls like paint cast off a brush. The defense did its best to present Iverson as helplessly troubled, the victim of childhood emotional abuse and neglect, but from his seat in the gallery it was clear to Connelly that the jury wasn't buying it. And so, when the judge handed down back-to-back life sentences with no chance for parole, nobody including Connelly was surprised.

A couple weeks after the sentencing, Connelly went to see Iverson in the county correctional unit where he was being held before his transfer to Angola. His hope was that looking the man in the eyes might yield some clarity, a chance to forgive, as he advised his own flock to do. However, as soon as the guards had stashed him in the windowless meeting room, used by attorneys to confer privately with their clients, his resolve began to flake away: regardless of what the Scriptures commanded, he didn't want to forgive this man. A jarring realization, but there it was—in spite of everything he was supposed to stand for, Connelly wanted to know that his own fury was righteous and just.

After nearly twenty minutes, the door clanked open and a handcuffed Iverson shambled into the room, dressed in a blue work shirt and pants that were at least two sizes too big. He was escorted by a towering, square-jawed guard, who shoved him into the metal chair on the other side of the bolted-down table, a bit more forcefully than seemed necessary, though Iverson didn't resist. Once the guard had retreated outside the door, a deadly silence fell over the room.

"Do you remember me?" Connelly said after a few moments.

"Does it matter?"

"I'm Allison Connelly's brother."

"If you say so." Iverson, who had the disinterested aspect of a student trapped in a lecture hall, adjusted his chunky prison-issue glasses, the cuffs clinking between his wrists. At forty-one, he was unremarkable in almost every way: not too tall or short, pasty-skinned with loose auburn curls, bulky but not unmuscular, the kind of person you would forget thirty seconds after meeting. Why this bothered Connelly, he wasn't sure. Someone murders your sister, you expect something monstrous, something beyond human. But there was nothing extraordinary about the man sitting across from him now. He was just that, a *man*, a far cry from the demonic entity the prosecution had propounded. "So, what do you want?"

"Honestly, I'm not sure," Connelly said.

"You come all this way and don't know why?"

"I want to know if you're sorry."

Iverson laughed, a throaty clucking noise. "That's what you're looking for, an apology?" He leaned toward Connelly as if to share a confession. "Fine, whatever. I'm sorry for what I did, okay? It wasn't personal."

Connelly rubbed his eyes, a headache simmering in the back of his skull. "Why did you do it?"

"I just wasn't in my right mind, is all I can tell you."

"Are you in your right mind now?"

"Think so, yeah."

At first, Connelly didn't even realize he had sprung out of his seat, not until he heard Iverson grunt in surprise as he gripped a fistful of his wavy hair while the fingers of his other hand wormed their way into the man's mouth to insert the folded up page from his bible, which he'd managed to finagle out of his pocket just before clamoring over the table. Iverson gagged and sputtered, though to Connelly's surprise he didn't struggle. Curiously, he seemed to accept being force-fed the slip of paper as part of his punishment, which was somehow worse than if he'd tried to defend himself, because it only intensified Connelly's crazed desire to see him suffer. *Fight back*, he thought, *give me a reason to hate you*. Even when the guard, alerted by the scuffling of chairs, glanced through the wire mesh window and then turned his back, leaving the mass murderer to be assaulted, Iverson didn't call for help. He just let Connelly cram the page down his gullet, docile as a circus animal.

Once the man had choked it down, coughing wetly into his bound hands, Connelly eased back into his seat, the blood still throbbing in his temples. All at once he felt ridiculous. How many times had he advocated that the suffering of good people was all part of a greater plan, something too vast and complex for the human mind to comprehend? How many times had he trotted out the stories of Job and Noah as evidence? Thinking about it now, watching Iverson spit a clump of soggy paper onto the tiled floor, made him feel stupid and deceitful, as though he'd been knowingly propagating a lie.

Breathlessly, Iverson said, "Anything else?"

But Connelly just sat there motionless, staring at the scuffed-up tabletop, his face the color of raw meat. Overhead, the caged fluorescents buzzed like insects. In a near-whisper, he said, "No."

Struggling up from the table, Iverson shuffled toward the door and called to the guard outside, "We're done in here!"

•

By the end of the week, the news of La Virgen Llorona had made national headlines, the camcorder footage having been picked up by several major networks, and Connelly had turned down nearly a dozen interview offers with nationally syndicated outfits. It wasn't just his adherence to the *Guidebook's* directives on media engagement—"the Ordinary shall express no public judgment unless authorized by the archdiocese"—but also the fact that he had yet to stumble upon a plausible explanation for the statue's tears. The sample he'd sent to the university lab in Lafayette had revealed very little, other than that the substance was chrism oil—olive oil mixed with balsam, used in confirmations. Available to anyone.

"You're famous," the waitress said when she arrived with his patty melt Friday evening, referring to the picture of him that had been aired on a talk show that morning, a headshot taken from the Shreveport diocese directory.

"I didn't have anything to do with that," he said. "They didn't ask me for permission."

"I take it the investigation isn't going well?"

"I wouldn't say that. There's just nothing to report."

"Is that a good thing or a bad thing?"

"Depends on what you believe, I guess."

A sizable portion of his afternoon had been spent on the phone with the statue's manufacturer, bouncing from one department to another until he managed to get ahold of a supervisor in the assembly plant. "And you say this thing is *crying*, is that right?" the man asked after Connelly had laid out the situation for him.

"In a manner of speaking, yes," he replied.

"What's that mean, 'in a manner of speaking'?"

"There is oil coming from the eyes, and we're not sure how. Could it have been trapped in the bronze?"

"Not likely. It would have been burned out in the heating process."

"So, you don't have any idea how this might be happening?"

The man let out a long breath, the sound of someone who had reached the end of his patience. And who could blame him? The whole thing was ludicrous, made even more so by the fact that divine intervention was becoming more plausible by the day. "I don't know what to tell you, sir. But it sounds to me like someone's jerking your chain."

Now the waitress set the covered plate down on the table and said, "Why don't you just break it open and look inside?"

"Can't. There are rules." Grabbing the *Guidebook* from the dresser, Connelly showed her the passage on page twenty-eight declaring that blessed objects were not to be wantonly destroyed in the course of inquiry, a violation of canonical law.

"Jeez, there's a guidebook for this?" she scoffed, flipping through the volume, which was fringed with multicolored Post-it tabs.

"There's a guidebook for everything."

"Okay, so then a drill, right? You could just cover the hole with bronze epoxy. No *wanton destruction*."

Connelly paused as he was lowering himself into his chair. "Bronze epoxy?"

"You didn't know about that?"

"No, I didn't."

The woman seemed amused by this. "You can order it over the phone, bronze epoxy and pigment. Cost you maybe ten dollars."

His sank into the chair as if he'd just been delivered life-changing news. Bronze epoxy. She made it sound so simple, so obvious. Like the answer to a child's riddle. Yet, instead of the gratification he might have anticipated, all Connelly could think about was his conversation with Father Ortiz days earlier, the breeziness in his demeanor. What was it the man had said? *Faith* is *reckless*.

"How do you know about this?" he asked the woman.

She shrugged as if the subject were too boring to pursue. "My stepdad was a welder. I know more about metal than I probably should."

"I wish you would have told me sooner."

The woman rested her arms on the room service cart. "Honestly, I figured you already knew."

•

In their final conversation, two days before Gary Iverson's attack on the Fort Worth DMV, Connelly and Allison had argued over the phone about their father, an eighty-two-year-old widower whose decade-long battle with dementia had left him unable to recall the names of his five children, let alone drive or shop for himself. More than once he'd wandered away from his home and gotten lost, only to be picked up by a squad car and taken to the station for Allison to retrieve. As the only sibling who still resided in town, she had spent the past several years as his sole caretaker, hauling him all over town for doctors' appointments, managing his arsenal of medications. Helping him to navigate his increasingly frequent bouts of senile paranoia.

And so, when Connelly, who had spent his share of time ministering in nursing homes, had suggested relocating him to an assisted living community, she'd balked: "I'm not going to just stick him in some home." The way she'd said "home" made it sound like a slur.

"It wouldn't be like that," Connelly said. "There are excellent facilities where he can get the care he needs."

"Meaning what, that I'm not providing it for him?"

"That's not what I'm saying, Allie. All I mean is that you can't do everything for him. You have your own life. There are specialists for this sort of thing."

"Why do you always think you know what's best for everybody?" Allison countered. "Like, we're all just begging for your guidance, is that what you think?"

Connelly cleared his throat, trying to keep his voice free of irritation. He could appreciate his sister's frustration; you put enough of yourself into something, it's irksome when someone suggests that your efforts are unsustainable. Nonetheless, he only had so much patience, and perhaps it spoke to their bond that she knew exactly how to expend it. "Allie, my job *is* to guide people."

"Sure, when they ask for it. But not everybody is looking to be saved. Believe it or not, some of us really are fine without your intervention."

The conversation ended shortly thereafter, Connolly lying about needing to return some phone calls before bed. The next morning, he found a message from her on the machine, recorded close to midnight. From the crooked lilt in her voice, it was clear she'd had a few glasses of wine: *"Hey, it's me. I just wanted to tell you that I'm sorry I lost my temper. I know you're just trying to help, and I appreciate it. I think we just have different ways of approaching problems, and that's okay. Anyway, call me back when you get a chance. Love you."* Only later, after the funeral, would he consider that it was his own guilt that prevented him from calling back right away. Because it wasn't her anger alone that had put him off—it was the fact that she'd been right about him.

•

Sitting across the desk from Father Ortiz, Connelly watched the portly priest finger his wooden cross in the absent manner of someone picking a scab. He described his conversation with the waitress, explaining how the two of them had spent fifteen minutes studying the three dozen photos, looking for some abnormality, something out of place. On some level, he'd hoped that she was mistaken, if only to justify the efforts he'd put into the inquiry thus far. And so, he was almost crestfallen when they finally spotted it on the top of the statue's head, a minor shift in texture like a long-healed scar, made almost invisible by the shadows—what he could only assume to be a blotch of painted-over epoxy. When Connelly, suddenly overcome by the accumulated fatigue of the past several days, had said he hoped he wasn't keeping the woman from her work, she'd scoffed. "Didn't you notice this place is dead? This is like the most interesting thing I've done in weeks."

From there, it wasn't hard to deduce the rest, how the heat had evaporated the oil inside the figure, trapping it in the plaster, allowing it to seep out through the pair of slits the perpetrator had scratched into the undersides of the eyelids, which were too small and well-concealed to be seen by the camera but which Connelly had discovered this morning during a reexamination.

"You'd make a hell of a detective," Father Ortiz commented when Connelly was finished walking him through the investigation.

"I'm just doing what they sent me to do." Between his knees, Connelly twisted the *Guidebook* into a tight coil. Sweat pooled against his lower back. "You haven't asked me who did it."

"Do I even want to know?"

"I'm thinking Mrs. Alvarez."

After the discovery, Connelly had gone back over the interview recordings. It wasn't what the woman had said but how she'd said it: her defensiveness, it seemed too manufactured, a put-on. This became especially apparent near the end of the conversation, when Connelly had asked her why she thought God would want to save her church in particular, out of the countless struggling houses of worship around the globe. On the recording there was a long period of silence, during which the woman had glanced at Father Ortiz, who nodded for her to go on. At the time, Connelly had thought nothing of this, but upon hearing it again something had clicked, like tumblers in a lock falling into place. Squaring back her small shoulders as if preparing for a brawl, the woman had said decisively, "You're wasting your time, Father Connelly. It is real. It is *not* a hoax."

Now Father Ortiz laced his fingers behind his head. "That's some accusation. Anna Lucia Alvarez is an old woman. I don't see how it's possible."

"It's not, unless she had help."

For a long period, neither of them spoke. Connelly held the man's eyes, a look that conveyed sympathy and recrimination at the same time. A tiny smirk played at the corners of the priest's mouth, the red plums of his cheeks bulging. It wasn't hard to see what made him such an effective cleric. Connelly had considered this late last night when, having resigned himself to sleeplessness, he'd climbed out of bed to stand at the hotel window, watching the traffic barrel down the cratered highway, past the dilapidated shops and restaurants, the vacant storefronts with their fractured panes. People headed to better venues. This wasn't the kind place you stayed if you had a choice—Father Ortiz understood this, just as he must have understood that faith was a shield: without it the world could crush you. Except, there was a reason the shield hadn't been used since the Middle Ages, wasn't there? It was too heavy and cumbersome, a liability on the battlefield.

"So, what now?" the man finally asked.

"Now I make my report to the archbishop."

"Am I out of a job?"

"That's not up to me."

"Do you think I should be?"

"You're asking the wrong guy."

"No, I don't think I am," Father Ortiz said. He clasped his hands on the desk, a teacher having a heart-to-heart with a troubled student. "I think you understand what we're trying to do here. And I think you can appreciate what will happen to these people if it's taken away from them."

Could he? It was true that Connelly had been almost sorry to have seen the patch of epoxy in the photograph. A part of him, he realized, had been holding out hope that the phenomena was authentic, a sign from above. Now, all he could feel was the same frigid numbness he'd experienced after Allison's burial, as though something precious had been taken from him by forces he was ill-equipped to confront. It was almost enough to make him divulge everything—his sister's murder, the trial, tearing the page out of his bible, his visit to Iverson in the detention center. Desperately, he wanted to unburden himself of it all, to unload everything he'd been lugging around this past year, and he could tell from the way the father was looking at him, like a man who knew all too well the value of confession, that he was ready to accept it.

But no, Connelly couldn't bring himself to confess, just like he hadn't been able to forgive his sister's murderer, because maybe not every resolution deserved to be celebrated. Some questions, it turned out, really were better left unanswered.

Instead, he muttered his thanks to Father Ortiz for his hospitality this past week, to which the man gave a knowing nod but said nothing, and then drifted into the sanctuary, where La Virgen Llorona loomed over the throng of worshippers, a gracious overseer. He shouldered his way through the bodies, issuing soft apologies each time he stepped on a toe or bumped an elbow, until he found himself standing in front of the statue, alongside folks curled up in praise like shuddering fists or gazing up at the Virgin with the open-mouthed wonder of children, the heaps of knickknacks on the floor resembling a street vendor's inventory.

It was as he was kneeling to deposit his rumpled copy of the *Guidebook*—the only thing he had left to offer now that he had run out prayers—that he heard the volume in the room plummet, the same kind of quiet that descends over a theater before a performance. Thick and full of expectation. Peering around behind him, Connelly saw that the roomful of disciples had turned its attention to him, their faces alight as they waited for his verdict. Slowly, he came to his feet, and with the same trepidation he always felt before a homily, he searched his mind for something to satisfy them, something that felt like it might be true.

Elliptical

As you enter your personal information into the LED console—male, sixty-five years old, two-hundred-forty pounds—you pretend not to notice the blonde in black stretch shorts and a pink halter pumping away on the machine next to yours. You are the Executive Vice President of Sales of an international grocery conglomerate, whose headquarters comprise a sprawling M-shaped complex on forty-five acres of pristine Tennessee grassland; in the aerial shots of the building hanging regally in the lobby, it appears as a single letter stamped onto an otherwise blank page. The gym is on the fourth floor of the complex, the cardio machines arranged in a long phalanx before the floor-to-ceiling windows. You guess the girl to be in her late twenties, fresh out of an MBA program and full of that hear-me-roar vitality. You can remember a time when the gym was exclusively male territory, not because women weren't entitled to their own means of exercise but because they posed a distraction from the decidedly unsexy business of working out.

Case in point: her outfit, which is the kind you can't even notice without anticipating a sexual harassment suit, and that's pretty much the last thing you need right now.

Not that you would even dream of making advances on a junior staff member. *Oh, how* gallant *of you!* Gail would tease, not necessarily kindly, you can just hear it, as if your concern over the girl's gym attire were anything more than a matter of prudence. Then she would ask why you don't just use the gym at the country club, away from all the work distractions. What she doesn't get is that you *like* the on-site fitness center. You like the state-of-the art equipment and the view of the hilly countryside afforded by the wall of windows. You like feeling connected to the rank-and-file, like you're all working toward the same goal.

There's something else, too. Women like this one always make you think of your own daughter Emily, twenty-four, also blonde, also heartbreakingly pretty, with her sparkling green eyes and her diminutive button nose. Or at least she used to be, before the accident at Wiley Lake two years ago. Since then she has been in a *persistent vegetative state*—a phrase the doctors insist on wielding like jackhammers—confined to an adjustable bed in the makeshift hospital suite in your living room. The bookshelves, once full of family photos, are now stocked with boxes of latex gloves and sani-wipes and gauze pads and a city of ointments and salves for her bedsores. She can move her fingers and tilt her head a few degrees, but beyond that she is completely immobile. Her young, lovely life frozen in limbo.

Your life, too, for that matter. When you're not at work you're at home with her, listening to the steady beeping of her heart monitor, draining her cranial shunt, cleaning the gunk from the corners of her mouth. Studying the lines of her beautifully slender face, mentally mapping them for when she's gone, which, if the doctors are to be believed, could be any time now. Except they've been saying that for a year and a half, so what the hell do they know? Certainly not enough to nurse her back to the waking world.

So no, you have no designs on the girl highstepping away on the elliptical next to yours. What you really want is to cover her up, throw a blanket around those bare shoulders like a Red Cross volunteer comforting a survivor of a natural disaster. Protect her as though she were your own.

The elliptical was Dr. Orr's idea, a low-impact way for you to manage your heart disease. With your broad chest and large bulldoggish head, you have always thought of yourself as more *sturdy* than *fat*. But your body doesn't work the same way it used to. In the past few months alone, you've managed to pack on an extra thirty pounds. How does that happen? Tragedy, you've discovered, has a way of skewing time, speeding up the aging process: one day you wake up and you're an oafish old man just trying to hold onto whatever is left. Emily used to say you were handsome, didn't look a day over forty. She was sweet like that. You wonder what she would say if she could see you now. Probably she'd lie, tell you you're still a looker, and you'd adore her for it.

Increasing the resistance to six, you think about the illustration the doctor showed you during your checkup a couple months ago, the pink cartoon arteries clogged with yellow plaque, and you recall how the bespectacled man had leveled a grim gaze and warned that you would need to make some serious lifestyle changes if you wanted to dance at your daughter's wedding. And no sooner had he said it than his eyes went as large as baseballs and his mouth fell open, horrified.

Jeez, I'm so sorry, Dr. Orr stammered. *I wasn't thinking.*

You, who have known the doctor for more than a decade, waved him off. The man had simply forgotten, that's all. He couldn't be expected to remember all his patients' life stories. Nonetheless, as you pretended to listen to the remainder of Dr. Orr's spiel, you couldn't ignore the glaring truth of the man's statement: there would be no wedding, no son-in-law to go deer hunting with, no sticky-fingered grandkids to twirl through the air like you used to do with Emily when she was a child, making her squeal with delight, her hair fragrant with that sweet loamy kid-scent. Like a handful of herbs plucked fresh from the soil. No legacy to continue. *A man's worth is no greater than the worth of his ambitions*, Marcus Aurelius said that, you read it on a quote-a-day calendar, and talk about someone who knew a thing or two about legacies.

Although, Marcus Aurelius had all of Rome behind him. But you? Who do you have? Your secretary Nina perhaps, a fortysomething waif who's been with you for just over eight years and whose notorious lack of people skills she makes up for with savant-level efficiency. But besides her, who? There was a time you could rely on your wife and daughter to be your support system, but those days are gone. You and Gail rarely speak anymore, and when you do it is usually about coordinating your schedules to look after Emily. (You have a home nurse who comes during the week, but Gail still refuses to leave her daughter for more than a few hours at a time.) You don't even share a bed anymore, not since Gail took to sleeping on the foldout sofa downstairs so she can be closer to Emily. Not that you fault her for this: you, too, feel a constant aching need to be near your daughter, despite the fact that most of the machines she's hooked up to are equipped with alarms in case her vitals drop. In fact, sometimes when Gail and the nurse aren't around you will sit beside Emily's adjustable bed and talk to her like you used to. Nothing of any consequence, just chatter about your day and the folks at work, projects you intend to complete around the house. You like to imagine that in some shadowy region of her brain she's processing what you're saying, that there's still some part of her that recognizes you.

You check the calorie counter: fifty-six so far. Not even a third of the chicken Caesar wrap you had for lunch. You up the incline to ten and the resistance to eight, and that's when the bolt of pain blasts through your chest like a blade bisecting your sternum. In a flash, all the breath vacates your lungs. You slump against the LED console, grappling for purchase, but your foot slips off the paddle and down you go, tumbling onto the floor in a tangle of limbs, the back of your head thwacking against the stiff, cracked matting.

Now you're on the floor gazing up at the beams crisscrossing the ceiling, and the pressure in your chest, Christ, it's like an eighteen-wheeler is parked on you. You sense that you've turned a corner toward death, and yet oddly your life doesn't flash before your eyes as the movies might have you believe. You aren't besieged by a wave of memories, friends and family and sunny beach vacations and birthday celebrations and long-forgotten lovers and bad decisions and irreversible mistakes. You don't think dejectedly about your wife of forty-four years, her thickly veined hands and thin, lank gray hair, the love between you that long ago degenerated into something hard and shapeless. Nor do you think about your invalid daughter in bed at home, her body wasting like an old car left to rust away in a field. Instead, your mind unaccountably zeroes in on one memory in particular: the crisp September evening one year ago that you drove to Wiley Lake.

Emily's accident had taken place six months prior. She had graduated from Vanderbilt and was home for the summer before she started law school. A few friends from high school had invited her out to the lake for an afternoon. Watching her descend the stairs in a pair of cutoffs and a bikini top, her towel draped around her pale shoulders like a shawl, you felt a peculiar combination of pride and embarrassment: you couldn't reconcile the coltish girl you knew with the radiant woman who now kissed you on the cheek and flounced out the door to where her friends were waiting for her in the driveway.

Wiley Lake was a large C-shaped basin in the foothills of the Great Smokey Mountains, a few miles outside of Pigeon Forge. For years visitors had lobbied the county for buoys to separate the swimming cove from the boating lanes, to replace the ancient, weathered pylons jutting from the water, half of which had toppled over and sunk, making it hard to determine where one area ended and the other began. This was how Emily and her friends, having swum out beyond the mouth of the cove, ended up in the path of an oncoming motorboat. The driver, as you would later learn, was a forty-five-year-old real estate agent who at the time had been too drunk to notice the girls bobbing in the water. Emily's friends would later attest that she had been floating on her back, so that she must not have heard the boat until the moment before it ran her over, the propeller blades severing two of her fingers and cleaving her skull open as cleanly as a machete. That she hadn't been killed was nothing short of a miracle, or so the doctors said.

However, after more than six months in the hospital, it became clear there was nothing more they could do for her, no more surgeries or procedures to jolt her from her coma, and so you and your wife were forced to move her home, into the living room suite. To make matters worse, because Emily had technically put herself in harm's way by swimming into a boating lane, and because the laws prohibiting the consumption of alcohol while operating a watercraft were rarely enforced, the judge had dismissed the case altogether.

Nothing miraculous about any that, as far as you were concerned.

And so this was how you found yourself following the dark winding highway out toward Wiley Lake one night a few weeks after the judge's decision. You had left work two hours earlier, stopping off at Bart's Tavern instead of going home, where one drink quickly turned into many, enough to fill you with a gloomy restlessness. You pulled into the graveled parking lot behind the manmade beach, exited the Buick and plodded across the cold sand. At the edge of the water, you stopped and stared out at the moonlight rippling on the surface. A vein of purple twilight lingered just over the ridgeline in the distance. In the air, the briny aroma of mud and algae.

As a father, everything that happened to your daughter came back to rest on your shoulders—this might have been the only thing in the world you knew to be true. And while it was unreasonable to think that you should have been there to save her from being mown down by the skiff, there it was all the same: the whole thing—the accident, the aborted trial—it all felt like a failure on your part. Something to atone for. So now you kicked off your shoes and stepped out of your slacks and peeled off your starchy oxford shirt, until you were standing in just your boxer shorts. You stepped into the water, your feet sinking in the muck, and then waded out as far as you could, the steely fall chill seeping into your bones. You swam out to where one of the remaining pylons jutted from the water like a crooked fang.

This was where it happened, you thought, the *incident* as your friends and family referred to it in conspiratorial whispers. Like an incantation. Lying back in the water, you stared up at the scrim of clouds passing over the moon and considered, not for the first time and not without a considerable degree of shame, whether you and Gail would have been better off if Emily had just died. While you would never admit as much to your wife, there was a part of you that wished she had, if only to spare her the indignity of her current state. Yes, your daughter was alive, and thank God for that, but it was only in a technical sense. She wasn't Emily, not anymore—would death have been any worse a fate?

How long did you float there? A half hour or so you guessed. Long enough for you to be startled out of your stupor when you heard the sound of tires crunching on gravel. You looked toward the beach to see a jeep with an arrowhead-shaped emblem on the door pulling up in the parking lot. A park ranger in green shirt and trousers climbed out and tromped down to the water's edge. He shined a flashlight in your direction.

Hey, you out there! he called. *Get out of there! You're not supposed to be here!*

You hesitated. To your left was the shore, but to your right was the expanse of the black lake. You could hear the water rippling in the silky darkness. Glancing back at the ranger standing with his hands on his hips, you began swimming further out into the lake. The man continued yelling at you, but you could barely hear him over your splashing. The water grew colder. In the dark, you could just make out the far side of the lake, about two hundred yards ahead. If you could just make it there to the opposite shore, things might begin to make sense again. You didn't know how, but it didn't matter. A distance to bridge, that's what you needed. Only, you were never a strong swimmer to begin with, and it wasn't long before you started to get winded, your breath coming in panicked gulps. Your arms, burning from the strain, locked up, and so did your legs. With no energy left to stay afloat, you flailed in the brackish water, which filled your throat and threatened to pull you down into its gullet.

That was when the ranger, still fully dressed, dashed into the lake and began breaststroking out to you. You felt his arms wrap around your chest in the middle of your thrashing. With what you would realize later must have been enormous effort, he hauled you back to shore and dragged you onto the sand, where he held you in his lap as you coughed up mouthfuls of brown water. You could feel his callused hand on your bare shoulder.

You're okay, you're okay. He spoke with the easy, reassuring lilt of a parent comforting a frightened child. *You're going to be just fine.*

Those words, they resound through your head as you lie on the floor of the fitness center, your field of vision clouded by the faces of concerned gym-goers—*Is he alright? What do we do?*—and you think that the elliptical is not unlike wading out into the lake, the way the slimy floor sucked your feet down so that every step was a test of strength. The back of your head aches from where you hit it on the ground. Probably going to be some laughs at your expense around the office tomorrow. Doesn't matter. The important thing is that you find a way up from the ground, out of the fitness center, away from all the bystanders gawking over the flabby old man whose body seems to be shutting down, but no, that eighteen-wheeler is still bearing down on your ribcage, making it impossible to maneuver.

Amidst the cluster of anxious faces the girl appears, shouldering her way into the scrum. Her bangs cling damply to her temples. She kneels down beside you.

Sir, can you hear me?

You try to respond but can't summon the words. She feels around your neck for a pulse, probes her fingers around in your mouth. Puts her ear to your lips to listen for breathing.

Call 911! she tells someone in the crowd. *Go! Now!*

Then she stacks her hands on your chest and begins the compressions, *One! Two! Three!*, and you are dimly—and absurdly—ashamed of how sweaty your t-shirt is.

Stay with me, okay?

The onlookers are watching the scene with the raptness of children, but you keep your eyes trained on the girl's.

One! Two! Three!

Her ponytail bouncing with each compression. She really does look like Emily, doesn't she? Same tapered chin, same vaguely protuberant forehead, which is maybe why you don't feel afraid, because you trust her. You trust her the same way you trusted the ranger, the way we trust those tasked with ushering us through our own calamities.

And then finally, after what could be seconds or years, you can no longer tell the difference—*breath*. Yes, slowly but surely, the truck is easing off you, the piercing sensation in your chest weakening, the air leaking back into your lungs. You can feel the blood returning to your face and limbs, warming your fingers. The girl pauses mid-compression as you take a long greedy gasp. Like you've just emerged from underwater. She presses two fingers to your neck, checks your pulse again. You breathe like it's your first time.

Don't try to move, she begins, but then stops short when your hand rises into the air, trembling like a needle pushing into the red, and seeks out her free hand. You interlace your fingers with hers and give it a few brief squeezes, just like you used to do with Emily, a game of yours, either person upping the number by one each time until the squeezes turned into a prolonged clutch. The way you might hold somebody's hand during a farewell. The girl is looking down at you like a puzzle she doesn't know how to solve, and you know that turning away from her would reignite the pain in your chest. Bringing her hand to your face, you press your cheek against the back of it, the edge of your jawbone nestling between two of her tiny knuckles, and you hold it there, waiting for her to tell you you're okay, you're okay.

Scream Queen

The Hell House Productions booth included a large vinyl backdrop featuring the company's logo: blood spatter affecting the shape of a haunted mansion. Lena imagined that the immense size of the logo made her look small by comparison, defenseless, sitting all alone at the foldable table with the backdrop behind her, before the loose line of bodies snaking out toward the other booths showcasing comic book artwork and movie paraphernalia. Horror aficionados eager for a twenty-dollar autograph. Her signing had been a last-minute addition to the convention schedule—this according to the youngish man with ear gauges and a lip stud who, minutes earlier, had fetched her from the supply closet the company had been using as a greenroom in the Mobile convention center. "We were supposed to have the dude from *Slaughterbots*, but he broke his leg skiing," he'd explained. "Anyway, I'm just so stoked you're here. I love *Psychosoul*. I don't think people have given the franchise a fair shake."

"I try not to listen to the critics," Lena lied.

"Okay well, you need anything? Water, coffee? They have awesome veggie wraps, want me to get you one?"

"I'm good, thanks."

"I'm gonna go ahead and get you one."

The image on the glossies was at least twenty years out of date, though if her fans noticed any discrepancy between the winsome, raven-haired vixen in the picture and the hard-faced woman behind the table, the skin beneath her chin beginning to sag like a turkey wattle, they kept it to themselves. Nonetheless, as she scribbled her name on one glossy after another, she couldn't stifle the familiar barb of revulsion she felt for them: even after thirty years in the entertainment business, she had never been able to stomach her fans' admiration. How could she, knowing that it had very little to do with her but with what she represented? Kitsch, the joyful lure of the ridiculous. She was an *attraction* to them, not a person. Still, at least she still had fans, she had to remind herself of this, which was more than you could say for some of the people she'd worked with. How many actors did she know who, after years in the business, had found themselves destitute, slogging away at supermarkets or restaurants or worse, ground up and spit out by the Hollywood machine? "We don't realize how lucky we are until our luck runs out," her AA sponsor Tracy was fond of saying, a font of corny truisms.

She was right, of course—Tracy usually was—but then she wasn't the one who had been roped into the panel discussion later that afternoon, "Behind the Mask: Remembering Jerry Hoag," star of the *Psychosoul* franchise. That was the real reason Lena was at X-Con, and she'd been dreading it ever since Hell House had called weeks earlier to beg for her participation. Her guess was that they needed a woman for diversity's sake and couldn't find another one with anything positive to say about Jerry. Not that Lena was brimming with accolades—in fact, she would have been happy to scour all her memories of Jerry Hoag from her brain like grime out of a bathtub. Unfortunately, money was tight these days, and she just wasn't solvent enough to refuse.

Of course, most of the pasty-skinned gawkers in the autograph line wanted nothing more than to know about Jerry, what kind of person he was, what it was like to work with him. "Wonderful," Lena would say with a neutral smile, absently scrawling her name on a photograph. "He was a terrific guy." She'd said the same thing to the woman she'd been sharing the greenroom with half an hour earlier. An older woman, seventies perhaps, with stenciled eyebrows and a clownish smear of ruby-colored lipstick, she wore a low-cut blouse that drew attention to her liver-spotted cleavage. Lena recognized her from a sci-fi television show that had run decades earlier, though she'd forgotten her name as soon as the woman had introduced herself after Lena had slumped into the room, weary and cranky from the flight out of LAX. "I only ever knew Jerry by reputation," the woman had told her.

"It definitely preceded him."

"You say that like it's a bad thing."

"Depends on the reputation, I guess." Was she giving too much away? Tacky though it may have been to slander the very man she was here to honor, it was hard to talk about Jerry without lapsing into invectives.

"My dear," the woman responded, futzing with her lustrous red hair, which Lena realized was a wig, "isn't that why we got into this business in the first place, to be known by reputation? Who the hell wants to be a regular person?"

•

The *Psychosoul* series was the saga of Simon Willow, a homicidal lunatic who, upon being executed for the gruesome murders of over fifty people, makes a deal with Satan to return to Earth to claim as many innocent souls as possible on the Big Man's behalf. Jerry, a rat-faced mantis of a man, with his spindly legs and arms that seemed out of proportion to the rest of his body, portrayed Simon. It was the perfect role for him, given his love of tastelessness, which was exceeded only by his love of women, and big surprise that most of Willow's victims were female. Lena had played Denise Pemberton, Willow's perpetual target, who always managed to thwart him in the third act, sending him back to hell until the next installment. Critics made comparisons to Jamie Lee Curtis in the *Halloween* franchise, and in fact in *Psychosoul 2: My Soul to Take*, in a twist that still struck Lena as ludicrous, it was revealed that Denise was Willows' daughter. However, those same critics were quick to point out that *Psychosoul* was simply a retread of well-worn horror territory of the *Halloween* variety, and that Lena didn't bring the same vitality to her character that Jamie Lee had to hers—a charge that Lena never denied, because vitality seemed like a lot to ask of a character who spent the bulk of each film half-naked, drenched in fake blood.

In any case, the films had made her a minor celebrity in the horror movie world, until Jerry's death in 2009 after a brief battle with stomach cancer, at which point the franchise was retired, *Psychosoul* becoming just another title cluttering up the DVD bargain bin at Walmart. She spent the next couple years scrounging up whichever bit parts she could get in what turned out to be a series of box office bombs. There was the Xerces epic ("A blank film screen would have been an improvement"—*Rolling Stone*), followed by *MechaSoldier* ("Too violent for anyone under 15, and too dumb for anyone over"—*The New York Times*), and then a host of others that eventually saw her devolve into a toxic asset, another washed-up scream queen. "What can I say, some stars dim sooner than others," her publicist had said not long before she'd stopped returning Lena's calls. "Just be glad you ever had one."

•

A hefty kid in a *Hello Kitty* t-shirt lumbered up to the table. "You're so awesome," he said by way of a greeting as he deposited a grimy bill in Lena's hand.

"Thanks. I appreciate that."

"But if I'm being honest, I liked you a lot more in *Life Support*."

Lena paused a beat. "Is that so?"

"Don't get me wrong, I love *Psychosoul*." He spoke with the rehearsed bluster of a professor delivering a lecture. "But *Life Support* just felt like a better vehicle for you. Really showcased your range. *Psychosoul* was a bunch of running and screaming a lot of the time. Didn't speak to your talents."

Lena had snagged the role of a wisecracking nurse on *Life Support* when she was twenty-three, a sitcom about a zany troupe of inner-city hospital employees. With only a single improv class under her belt, she was surprised at how adept she was at physical comedy, all the pratfalls and hokey sight gags. Even now, more than two decades later, she regarded her time on the show, which had lasted five seasons before its cancellation, with the same wistfulness some people regard a first apartment, a place where you begin to figure out who you are. Sometimes she even found herself humming the frustratingly catchy theme song, especially in moments of doubt, of which there had been plenty over the course of her career: *Every now and then we all need a hand/ Every now and then we all come up short/ So call on me/ if you ever need a little life support!*

Lena studied the kid. She put him somewhere around sixteen, his face still fleshy with baby fat, a snatch of greasy fuzz beneath his hooked nose. Another self-professed movie expert compensating for a lack of social skills. It must have been quite the power trip for him, unloading his opinions like a shrewd producer offering notes. Horror devotees were notoriously zealous, although she had never figured out how to feel about her fans' fervent devotion to an institution that was, when you really got down to it, a lie. Movies weren't truth—they might have been *about* truth, but they weren't truth themselves. So it was aggravating, sure, the kid's unflappable certainty, though not nearly as aggravating as knowing that he was right, *Life Support* had been the more rewarding role.

Summoning a smile, Lena dashed off her name on the glossy, the marker squeaking like a rodent. "Thanks for stopping by," she said in the sugary sweet tone she reserved for these events. Then she called for the next person in line.

•

The truth was that Lena had never liked Jerry. He was loud and brash and crude, the kind of guy who told off-color jokes and then insisted on explaining why they were hilarious. On set he was known for walking around with a rubber dildo hanging out of his pants, a gag he seemed to think was as timeless as a hand buzzer or knock-knock jokes. He would pretend to stumble into the female crew members, pressing it against their thighs, prompting them to giggle obligingly for fear of ending up on his bad side. That Jerry Hoag was irreplaceable and therefore not to be crossed was well-known to everyone, and any extras who complained about his behavior—and over the years Lena had seen plenty—were usually dismissed from the set, shuffled off like bums from a doorway.

And while Lena had been aware of this for years and had put up with her own share of Jerry's misconduct, it wasn't until *Psychosoul 5: Blood Oath* that she'd finally mustered the courage to speak to Kurt, the director, about Jerry's constant pawing at her. The filming had taken place on a West Virginia farm comprising a broad, sprawling hillside and lush pine forest. The first scene shot featured Lena, in nothing but a cropped t-shirt and skimpy shorts, wriggling out of Willow's grasp before sprinting off into the trees. It was 3 AM, starless, the temperature hovering in the forties, making her breath visible, better for shooting. The whole thing felt eerily punitive, the one-time Emmy nominee for Outstanding Actress in a Comedy Series, now on the far side of forty—ancient by Hollywood standards—reduced to just one more busty bimbo struggling to stay relevant.

"That's just Jerry being Jerry," Kurt replied, as though they were talking about a rambunctious toddler and not a fifty-three-year-old actor.

"It's unprofessional," Lena protested. "I'm getting a bruise from all his pinching."

"What do you want from me? The guy *is* the franchise."

Lena continued to steel against Jerry's increasingly bold fondling the best she could, because she desperately needed the work, until take fourteen when, likely interpreting her restraint as invitation, he went so far as to swipe his hand between her legs. Out of instinct, she launched an elbow into his face. It connected with a soft crunch against his nose, like snow grinding beneath a boot. Jerry flailed backward, whacking his head against a tree, his pained squeals garbled by the grotesque costume prosthesis (as a minion of hell, Simon had been outfitted with a sadistic metal cage over his face that kept all his orifices open as if in a perpetual state of unearthly horror, though in reality it was just foam rubber). Lena, bolstered by her own impetuousness, tromped to the dressing tent to grab her clothes, ignoring Kurt's pleas for her to please just be reasonable, and then climbed into her rented Hyundai to speed back to the shabby motel where Hell House had stashed the cast for the duration of the shoot.

•

"I don't know how many more of these I can do," Lena said, her phone sandwiched between her ear and shoulder while she struggled to light a cigarette against the breeze. From the brick terrace on the backside of the convention center, she looked out over the sludgy gray Mobile River, running through the heart of town, south toward Mobile Bay. The late June sun was scalding, the air thick as steam. Other smokers stood nearby in clusters, casting furtive glances in her direction. She'd gotten similar looks when she'd gone strolling through the convention after the signing, perusing the anime illustrations and video game exhibitions, the flabby vendors pedaling action figures and bobble-heads—folks gawping at her, probably recalling her semi-nude scene from the first *Psychosoul* film, yet unable to put a name to the face. "I know I should be grateful to these people for giving a shit, but it just feels like I'm being lobotomized."

"A lobotomy doesn't have to be a bad thing," Tracy replied. "I wouldn't mind parts of my brain being removed."

"Then come to Alabama. You'll have a wild time."

"Are you doing your breathing exercises?"

"Yeah."

"Bullshit."

"Then why ask, Tracy?"

On the other end of the phone, Lena could hear the woman's eleven dogs yapping in the background. After getting sober, Tracy had started volunteering at animal shelters; with no children of her own, she said it gave her something to think about other than herself. Trouble was, she couldn't visit a shelter without coming home with a new critter to look after: in addition to the dogs, she had seven cats and two ferrets that roamed the house freely, nesting in piles of dirty laundry. Every time

Lena went to Tracy's place, she left with the stink of wet fur embedded in her clothes. Some people, it wasn't hard to see how they ended up turning to the bottle, but then wasn't that the thing about alcoholics: it actually had very little to do with the booze.

Lena went on, "I'm just so tired of it, these conventions. It's not why I got into this."

"Why did you get into it?"

"To be a star, to be famous," she replied as if this were the most obvious fact in the world. She thought about the woman from the greenroom: *Who the hell wants to be a regular person?*

"You sort of are famous."

"I'm a B-movie actress a few years shy of sixty. I'm not famous, I'm a curiosity."

"Better than being nothing at all," Tracy offered. "Anyway, it's just a job, and you like your job for the most part, don't you?"

Did she? She had at one point, but now she couldn't say. For that matter, what *was* Lena's job? To call her an actress might have been a stretch; these days she made more money from convention appearances than she did from her infrequent walk-ons in the straight-to-video slasher flicks that had become her staple. Some people would have said this was a good thing—she was still making a living, wasn't she, still acting? But those people were probably washouts themselves who, like Lena, would never reach the level of acclaim they'd once dreamed of. Didn't know what the hell they were talking about.

Lena took one last drag and flicked her half-smoked cigarette into the river. "Sure," she said.

"Then just do your best to get through it, and go to your hotel and take a hot bath, order take-out. Spoil yourself a little." Tracy hollered for the dogs to quiet down. "Just remember, the things we love tend to come the hardest for us."

As Lena was stowing her phone in her purse, a teenager with chunky glasses and an Adam's apple like a golf ball broke off from one of the packs of spectators and sidled over to her. "I love your scream," he said, his voice a near-whisper, almost inaudible over the wind. Behind him, his friends tittered. Clearly, he'd been put to the confession. "I could listen to it all day."

"Well," Lena said, slathering her lips with Chapstick and then pivoting to return inside, "let's hope it never comes to that."

•

After storming off the *Psychosoul 5* set, Lena had sped back to the motel and commenced getting blindingly drunk. What was it about motel rooms that always aroused the need to self-abuse? Maybe it was what they embodied—a halfway point, a place where nothing is permanent. This one was a sickly shade of green, with water stains on the ceiling and an AC unit that clattered like a boat motor and a dingy minifridge barely big enough to accommodate a six-pack. Not that it mattered; she'd already gone through that day's supply of beer. By that point in her career she was throwing back four or five first thing in the morning and then spending the rest of her day sneaking slugs of vodka or wine, enough to maintain a baseline buzz. Which made it hard to account for her actions sometimes; losing days at a stretch wasn't uncommon for her, and in fact she wondered if she would even remember clocking Jerry. It was a memory she would like to hold onto, even if the company fired her for assaulting the star of the picture. Except they were already a month into shooting, and it would cost too much to replace her at this point. Not to mention that any damage to Jerry's face would surely be obscured by the prosthesis. No, she'd just have to show back up tomorrow, square things with Kurt, and hope that Jerry had learned his lesson.

By the time the knock at the door came, she had almost polished off the bottle of pinot grigio she'd purchased at a gas station. Peering through the peephole, she was all at once convinced that she was hallucinating. It was the only way to explain what she saw: Jerry, leaning against the frame, dressed in sweatpants and a t-shirt that said *SARC: MY SECOND FAVORITE -ASM*. A large white bandage covered his swollen purple nose, which the lens warped into something monstrous.

Lena cracked the door as much as the chain would allow. "What do you want?"

"A peace offering," he said, hoisting a handle of scotch.

She peered at the bottle like a person dying of thirst eyeballing a glass of water. It was close to 11 PM. The wine was almost gone, and in her anger she hadn't stopped to pick up anything else to drink.

"Not interested," she said.

"It's good stuff. I got it in Scotland, a little town outside of Inverness."

"I know where scotch comes from, Jerry."

"Ah, but this is magic scotch, you see. It resolves conflict, makes people's differences disappear." He made a fluttering gesture with his fingers like a magician performing a coin trick. Then, reading the apprehensive look on her face, added, "Seriously, I'll be good, I swear. Just wanted to clear the air."

Lena cast one more look at the bottle, that smooth caramel shade. She could feel her resolve dissipating, the twisted black craving thrumming in her skin like an illness she couldn't shake. Would she be able to make it through the night without any alcohol? She didn't know, but now didn't seem like a good time to test that possibility. She could stomach Jerry for a little while if it earned her a few drinks.

Removing the chain, she ushered him into the room. Folding his lanky body into one of the two padded chairs flanking the table, he poured them each a couple fingers of scotch into paper coffee cups.

Holding up his cup, he said in a singsong voice, "Here's to you, and here's to me, the best of friends we'll ever be. And if we ever disagree, well fuck you and here's to me." He threw back his drink.

"Cute."

"Look, I'm not a prince, I get it. I can be an asshole sometimes."

"Am I supposed to applaud you for acknowledging that?" said Lena, sitting across from him on the edge of the bed. Downing her drink, savoring the heady sting in her gullet, she held out her cup for another round. "I mean, what do you want, a gold star?"

Jerry gave them each a refill. In the begrudging tone of someone unaccustomed to owning up to his foibles, he said, "I suppose I do owe you an apology."

"I'd say so."

"Fine, I'm sorry. But you did fuck up my nose pretty good." As if to drive the point home, he brought his fingers to the bandage, wincing at the touch. "So I'd say we're even, wouldn't you?"

"If you can keep your hands off me, sure."

"What can I say? I'm an affectionate guy."

Lena tossed her back her slug of scotch. "Then get a dog."

They drank in silence for a few moments, the muffled din of televisions in other rooms the only sound. It occurred to Lena that, even after having filmed four movies with each other, this was the first time she and Jerry had been alone together. Most of their scenes they filmed separately, the shots spliced in together in the editing room, so up until now they had never had the occasion to speak one-on-one. She felt her body going numb, her nerves deadening mercifully as the booze did its work. What was it Dean Martin had said about people who didn't drink? *When they wake up, that's as good as they're going to feel all day.* A nice line, although it was probably easy to be glib about such things when you were a member of the Rat Pack, someone with clout. But Lena, who was she? Just another nearly broke actress sitting around a dirty motel room, still waiting for her shot after all these years. A walking cliché, that's what she was. Only years later, after she'd gotten sober, would she realize she hadn't been drinking to feel good, she'd been doing it to feel nothing at all.

"I'm not a bad guy, you know," Jerry said.

"I didn't say you were."

"But that's what you think."

"Why do you care what I think, Jerry?"

"Because," he replied, downing yet another finger of scotch, "I respect you. We've worked together for years. I think you're a terrific actress."

Lena looked away, at a loss. Jerry had never complimented her before. Or anyone, that she knew of. It just wasn't part of his character. Was he really attempting to make amends, or was this all some sort of ploy? Either way, his earnestness made her uneasy. It was like a screaming baby suddenly going silent.

"I appreciate that, Jerry."

"Well, I mean it."

"Means a lot."

Another round of pours. "Actually, I think you could be fantastic. Like, really huge."

"That so?" Lena said.

"I've been doing this a long time. I know people. Good people. Things could work out really well for you."

That was when his gangly hand found its way to her thigh, gently kneading the flesh above her knee.

At first Lena didn't move. Surely this was another one of his bad jokes. It seemed so absurd, *so* unbelievably Jerry, that it couldn't have been for real—he must have been poking fun at his own lecherousness. But no, she could see it in his eyes, that hunger, dark and coarse, his fishy lips twisted into a smile like a badly healed scar. The look of a man used to getting what he wanted. Only it wasn't *her* he wanted, it was the conquest, the vindication. Screwing her would have been like exacting revenge for what she'd done to his face. With men like Jerry, everything always boiled down to pride.

Holding his gaze, she leaned forward as if to kiss him. She placed her hand on top of his. "Well, you and your friends?" she said, wrenching it off her leg, that impish grin falling from Jerry's face. "You can go fuck yourselves."

•

Gaudy dauphine chandeliers the size of Jacuzzis hung overhead in the massive ballroom where the panel discussion was being held, casting the three hundred or so audience members in an unsettling yellow glow, as though the light was being filtered through a puddle of urine. Lena sat at a train of tables at the front of the room, alongside nearly a dozen actors and directors and writers who had all worked with Jerry in one capacity or another. A number of them had had a hand in one or more *Psychosoul* pictures, though the only one she knew personally was Kurt. He'd strolled up to her as the audience was still streaming into the room, the other panelists mulling around, swapping stories about Jerry. In his oversized jean shorts and loud Hawaiian shirt, it wasn't a stretch to envision him as a rodeo clown. "Lena, how you doing?" he said, clamping her in a one-handed hug. Lena returned it with a businesslike pat on the back.

"No complaints, you?"

"Pretty good. Been awhile, huh?"

"Yep, long time." *Not since I was run off the set of Psychosoul 5*, she wanted to retort, but that felt petty, juvenile. She'd made a promise to herself to be mature, and so she was content to let the tension between them remain unspoken.

They chatted for a couple minutes, about the convention and the perils of flying out of L.A. and the muggy Deep South weather, anything but the subject of Jerry, before Kurt, taking on the contrite air of a student who had been caught cheating, finally broached it. "So, would I be a total dick if I said I was surprised to see you here?"

"You really want me to answer that?" Lena said.

"I guess not."

"We all gotta work, Kurt."

"Is that what this is for you, work?"

"What else would it be?"

"Seems like punishment to me," he said. "To be honest, I don't know why you'd put yourself through it."

"Jesus, Kurt. I'm trying to be an adult here."

Now, a few minutes after three o'clock, the moderator, the second lead in a Netflix series about a family of cannibals, sauntered up to the podium to get the presentation started. "Jerry had one of the most eclectic careers of anyone I've ever known," he said into the mike, his voice booming out across the packed room, all those acne-plagued faces watching with the raptness of parishioners at the feet of a bible-thumping minister, "and he left behind a wealth of cinematic delights." As he droned on, a gallery of behind-the-scenes snapshots of Jerry played on the giant projection screen behind the panelists. Jerry with a mouthful of Skittles. Jerry pretending that his hand was a chest-bursting alien. Jerry, in full prosthesis, riding a bike in a lot behind a sound stage. Jerry laughing uproariously at a joke. The images were silly and charming, a tender depiction of a much-loved icon. When the moderator was finished with his remarks, the panelists began offering up their own sappy requiems:

"—a gentle spirit with a huge heart."

"—hilarious, one of the funniest people I've ever met."

"—not an unkind bone in his body."

"—really carved a path for character actors. I mean, as far as movie monsters go."

Were they really this enamored with him, or like her were they putting up a front to disguise their distaste for the man? Lena supposed that neither option was any better. Regardless, she managed to get through the tribute without adding more than a few bland words of praise—"One of a kind," "He really had a presence"—after which the moderator opened the discussion up to questions. Audience members filed down to the microphone at the front of the room. Not surprisingly, they all wanted to know about the future of *Psychosoul*. Would there ever be another one? Which one had been Jerry's favorite? How long did his makeup take? With her hands clasped demurely on the table, Lena, trying to appear as congenial as possible, let the other panelists field the questions, smiling and laughing at all the appropriate moments. The picture of absolute professionalism. Yet, she couldn't ignore the queasy wave of anxiety building in her gut, as though she'd found herself in a position for which she was grossly underqualified. It was the same feeling she'd had during her first few auditions after moving to L.A., like any second she would be outed as a fraud.

Someone wanted to know how much input Jerry had on the scripts. "He loved to improvise," Kurt responded. "Sometimes he would come up with lines of his own, and we'd keep them in. Like the part in *Three* when Simon licks Denise's face and says 'I can't wait to suck your soul'? That was all Jerry. We just thought it was great, so we left it."

He glanced toward Lena at the opposite end of the tables as if awaiting her approval. But she was lost in thought about her early showbusiness days, those grand greenhorn years, when there was still plenty to hope for and so little to fear. She'd dropped out of college to move to L.A., even though her acting experience up to that point amounted to only a few high school plays and a church-sponsored production of *Our Town*. But Lena had grit, or so it had been intimated to her in ways that weren't exactly complimentary, which, as far as she could tell, was most of what you needed to succeed. And so when the *Life Support* role had come along, this only confirmed that she was on the right track.

She thought about the day of their first promo shoot for the program in a studio in Glendale, the photographer guiding the six main cast members, most of them ingénues, through a series of quirky poses—arms resting on each others' shoulders, back-to-back buddy-buddy style. Afterward they had gone for a celebratory lunch at a Mexican restaurant and gotten wasted on margaritas. It was the beginning of something monumental, they could all feel it, something that would change them forever. Were they naïve for not considering that everything, even the really big things you spend your whole life waiting for, are all temporary? Not necessarily. Who can entertain such thoughts when you're staring down the barrel of stardom?

Looking at Kurt now, she could feel the audience's collective gaze trained upon her like a gunsight, waiting for her input.

"It definitely caught me off guard!" she said finally, playing along. Wasn't that what she was getting paid to do? Dutifully, the crowd chuckled.

•

She was so hungover the morning after her encounter with Jerry that it didn't even arouse her suspicions when, upon arriving to the set, Kurt pulled her aside as she was heading for the makeup trailer. "Need to have a word," he whispered. Probably he just wanted to harangue her for her assault on Jerry the previous day—which, fine, let him get it over with so she could get into her ridiculous costume. Looking back, she should have been alerted by his grim look, like a doctor preparing to deliver devastating news, or by the anxious, tight-lipped glances of crewmembers scuttling about.

"Didn't they call you?" he asked when they were out of earshot.

"Who?"

"The studio. You didn't talk to them?"

She told him that she hadn't gotten around to checking her messages yet, though the truth was that in her liquor-addled state it just hadn't occurred to her. "Why, what's the deal?"

"They want to take the movie in a different direction."

"What the hell does that mean, 'a different direction'?"

Nervously, Kurt cleared his throat. "It means you should probably see about getting a flight home."

Watching the portly director shift uncomfortably under her gaze, Lena could see that he was lying. And it didn't take a genius to figure out why. This was Jerry's doing, a final *fuck you* to her for rebuffing his advances. She should have known that Hell House would do whatever it needed to keep him happy, even if it meant cutting her and reshooting the entire thing. And the worst part? It was her word against his—no one would ever believe her, or care, because he was Jerry Hoag, the star. *The guy* is *the franchise.*

"Where is he?" she growled.

"Where is who?" Kurt said.

"You know who the fuck I'm talking about, Kurt! Don't pull that shit!"

He rubbed the back of his thick neck. "It's probably not a great idea for you to talk to him right now."

"So, you're okay with this?"

"Lena," he sighed, "I just do what I'm told. I don't like it, but what am I going to do? You know as well as anyone how these things work."

•

By the time the scrawny girl with neon pink hair approached the microphone, Lena was almost certain she was going to crawl out of her skin. The panel had been going for over an hour, and the moderator didn't appear to be in any hurry to wrap it up, not with the cavalcade of folks still waiting to lob out their questions. She needed a cigarette, and she needed to get back to her room and ditch her grungy clothes, and she needed the hell out of Alabama. The girl had tiny elfin features, and she sported a lacquering of black eye makeup that only made her seem young and vulnerable. Another kid desperately striving to be seen as an adult. Whether this was what caused the audience to go silent, or the fact that she was the only female so far who had ventured to ask a question, Lena couldn't be sure. Probably both.

"This is a question for Lena," the girl said, her voice as soft as tissue paper.

Lena cleared her throat. "Go ahead."

The girl tucked a hank of hair behind her ear. "Okay, well, it's kind of weird, maybe. I read somewhere that you and Jerry had a falling out and that's why you didn't do *Psychosoul* 5. I was just wondering if that was true."

Out of her periphery, Lena noticed the other panelists' heads swivel in her direction. Her departure from the movie had been documented on a number of prominent horror blogs, though by that point the franchise's popularity was waning, and her feud with Jerry—that was how they phrased it, a *feud*—just wasn't interesting enough to garner any traction. In spite of the online outcries from a handful of diehard fans, the story was forgotten in a couple weeks, like it had never happened. Like *she* had never happened.

Nevertheless, a rumble now ran through the crowd, as though the girl had made a severe faux pas. And by their rules, Lena supposed she had. They were here to honor Jerry, not to dredge up drama from the past.

But despite her initial skittishness, the girl didn't appear fazed. There was something determined about her, stalwart. This was why she was here, to ask this one question, and Lena, much to her own surprise, was bolstered by her fortitude, breaching protocol in front of all these Jerry Hoag fanatics, in search of the truth. Because after all, wasn't that why they were here, to learn the truth about him, the kind of man he was? Weren't they all joined in the same mission?

Yes—here it was, her opportunity to come clean about what had happened. To at long last salvage her name.

"Jerry was..." she began. Jerry was *what*? An asshole? A pig? "He was complicated."

Only, as she looked back into the girl's dusky eyes, it dawned on her that maybe her name wasn't worth salvaging, not anymore. And honestly, was it ever? Who would benefit from the truth? Certainly not the girl herself, who was watching Lena now with the somber anticipation of someone who hopes that she's wrong but suspects better, and certainly not the hundreds of other faces peering up at her, wanting to believe that their hero was exactly that, someone who could never let them down. Because Jerry *wasn't* complicated. People generally weren't. They wanted what they wanted and they would do whatever they could to get it. But if there was one thing Lena had learned from her years on-screen, it was that the truth is messy and painful and usually not worth the effort it takes to uncover it. Moreover, it seemed to go against the spirit of the convention. Weren't they all here, herself included, because they felt that the real world was a little *too* real?

At some point in her forestalling she noticed a look of bewilderment come over the faces of the crowd, not unlike the look that Jerry had given her when she'd pried his claw from her leg, and it was then that she realized she was humming. A soft single note that issued steadily from her throat like air from a leaking tire, building in volume. She could feel it rising from someplace deep in her gut, involuntary, as though it was somehow being drawn out of her, making it impossible to speak, although as she stared back at the girl, she was all at once certain that to stop now would be to sacrifice something precious.

Finally, once the humming had risen to a crescendo, Lena belted out, *"Every now and then we all need a hand! Every now and then we all come up short! So call on me if you ever need a little life support!"*

She sang with the fervor that had characterized her years on the show, and for an instant it was almost as if she was back there, on the *Life Support* set, a blessedly guileless kid. She even *dum-dum-dummed* her way through the bridge, much to the dismay of the other panelists, who observed the spectacle the way one might watch a tragedy unfold. But Lena didn't care. Nor would she care later on, after the incident had been hashed over in the blogs—*"SCREAM QUEEN TURNS SONGBIRD AT X-CON"*—and, shortly thereafter, when the few directors and producers with whom she still had good relationships began to distance themselves from her, as though she'd lost her mind. Because in a way, maybe she had, and maybe that wasn't so terrible. Perhaps Tracy had been onto something—*I wouldn't mind parts of my brain being removed.* Who knew which pieces of the self were worth holding onto? All that mattered now was that Lena kept singing, ignoring the moderator's quip about the panel having turned into *American Idol*, all the while watching the girl, who was grinning as if to say *I hear you*, as she mouthed the words along.

Inverse Functions

The mortician has gone overboard with the embalming fluid, and Mr. Harmon's rouge-caked face has the swollen, bulbous character of an overripe pumpkin. Dressed in a grey suit with a purple pocket square, his once unruly beard trimmed to a fine fuzz, he looks nothing like the dumpy oaf that Eric took for Trig in 1998, who favored short-sleeved button-downs and ketchup-stained khakis. Eric was sixteen at the time, the kind of middle-of-the-road student who teachers love trying to turn into a success story, something to brag about over reheated lasagna in the lounge. "You're your own worst enemy," the man once told him during an after-school tutoring session. "You keep getting in your own way. Stop telling yourself you can't do it and just do it."

It was this sort of matter-of-factness that endeared Mr. Harmon to his students, as evidenced by the forty or so former ones—most of whom appear to be in their thirties, a few years younger than Eric—scattered around the room swapping anecdotes, like how he used to stand on the desk when he lectured about derivatives, or the time he received a broken nose while trying to break up a brawl in the classroom. A few of them are misty-eyed, their voices tinged with awe-struck reverence, as though it's a celebrity they're talking about. He has yet to join the line of well-wishers, partially because he's never known what to say in these situations; when it comes to funerals he's always felt out of place, like he's somehow complicit in the person's death.

Mostly though, it's because he's not entirely sure why he's here. To pay his respects certainly, but more than that he needs to satisfy his crazed desire to see the man's body. It had been simmering in him, this desire, ever since his mother forwarded him the obit three days ago. There is also the issue of his being put on indefinite leave from the pharmacy, which made getting out of town for a few days seem like a sensible idea.

All of which is why he's made the five-hour trek to Roanoke. His plan was to slink into the funeral home, get a look at the corpse, and then quietly make his exit before the sixty milligrams of oxycontin that he snorted this morning begins to wear off.

But there's something else. He had also hoped to see Austin Mackey, his best friend from junior year—a foolish hope, he supposes, given that Austin never seemed to care much for Mr. Harmon, though Eric never understood why. They'd met in Mr. Harmon's class, second period. Both of their fathers had died around the same time two years prior—Eric's from lymphoma, Austin's from a pulmonary embolism—which gave them something to bond over. Because Austin's mother, a low-level county government drone, was usually gone until early evening, and because neither he nor Eric had any interest in extracurriculars, they spent most of their afternoons in Austin's basement playing ping-pong or watching MTV. For Austin, it was a friendship of utility: Eric's devotion imbued him with a sense of eminence, like an older brother abiding a younger sibling, even though he was four months Eric's junior. To say Austin was Eric's first real crush might be technically correct, though he didn't recognize this at the time, as he had only just begun to come to grips with his sexuality. Austin had dark hair terminating in a sharp widow's peak and big ears that stuck out like handles. While he wasn't particularly handsome, there was a devil-may-care quality in his homeliness, an intimation that it was intentional. Were it not for the half-assed cleft palate surgery that had left his top lip flattened and scarred, costing him any chance of joining a higher-status clique, he wouldn't have had anything to do with Eric, who was just happy to be with someone as awkward and unpopular as he was. It was Austin who had first started the joke about Mr. Harmon's daughters, visible in the photos the man kept on his desk. "Those bitches look like Neanderthals," he'd quip, "'Og and Trog want dick! Give us dick!'" Cruel though the bit might have been, that never stopped Eric from cackling wildly, if only to appease his friend. It made it easier to stomach Austin's ribbing about his tutoring sessions with Mr. Harmon, as if they were Eric's idea to being with.

Now Austin is nowhere in sight, and before Eric is able to escape, he spots Ashley Carmichael making her way toward him through the crush of bodies. She is accompanied by a man Eric presumes to be the new husband, a bearish brute with a graying crewcut whose navy blazer—*navy!*—strains at the shoulders and across his chest, whom she leads by the hand like a child. He's the kind of person Austin would have scoffed at, and again Eric wishes his old friend were here to join in his contempt.

"Eric!" she squeals, enveloping him in a polite embrace. "Oh my god, it's so good to see you!" In high school she was mousy and unsmiling, always skulking the halls with her books clutched to her bony chest as though she feared they might be ripped away, her face hidden behind the curtain of her greasy hair. However, the years seem to have been kind to her: gone is the long hair, replaced by a tasteful bob that is more suited to her face's diamond shape, and she appears to have put on a few much-needed pounds. She is wearing a sleeveless black dress with a plunging neckline that, in its showcasing of her clavicle, comes perilously close to inappropriate.

She introduces the husband, Grant or Stan or Cliff, something predictably monosyllabic that Eric forgets right away. The man regards him with the disinterest of someone watching a waiting room television. A moment later, he excuses himself to go sign the guestbook.

He and Ashley make obligatory small talk. Or rather, Ashley does. She manages a beauty parlor, has three kids with the husband. Is getting her realtor's license. Just started yoga. Eric struggles to keep his face arranged into an expression of interest, though it's difficult; is there anything more patronizing than small talk? Will used to call him a snob for his inability to stomach idle chitchat. "Why is it so hard for you to pretend to give a shit about anyone other than you?" he sniped at him once on the drive home from a Christmas party hosted by his boss, during which Eric had yawned loudly in the midst of a coworker's tale about her Lyme disease diagnosis.

"I was just tired," he argued.

"These are our friends."

"They're *your* friends. I don't know these people."

"All the more reason for you to act like a grownup. They matter to me."

"Oh, well if they matter to *you*."

Will hooked a sharp right onto their street. Eric had to grip the door handle to keep from toppling over. "I'm allowed to have other people in my life. Maybe you should try it, too."

Now Ashley shifts the conversation to him. Where is he living? Baltimore. Is he married? God no. Job? Pharmacist—which is still technically true, since he hasn't been officially let go, not until the state licensure board concludes its investigation.

"Wow, a pharmacist," Ashley says, feigning intrigue the way people do whenever Eric discusses his job. To them he's somewhere between a medical professional and a stooge for the insurance companies. "Weird to imagine you behind that little counter, mixing potions or whatever."

"Why?"

"I'm not sure. I guess it's just hard to think of you as anything other than Austin's friend. We're all so grown up, you know?"

When Ashley came along their junior year, everything between Eric and Austin had changed practically overnight. The whole thing seemed abrupt—one day she was just *there*, in the basement with them, like she'd been there the whole time and Eric had overlooked her. What Austin saw in her, Eric had no clue and wasn't about to ask, but it felt like a betrayal all the same. Most days she and Austin would cuddle together on one end of the sofa, murmuring to each other, while Eric sat in his usual spot on the other end brooding over her intrusion. To Ashley's credit, she did sometimes try to include him in their conversations, but Eric always got the sense that it was out of pity and so he kept his responses perfunctory and cold.

If either of them ever picked up on his resentment, however, they never let on. Nor did they say anything when his visits to Austin's house became less frequent and then, by the end of the year, stopped altogether. By the time they graduated, they were practically strangers to each other again. Austin and Ashley married out of high school, only to find themselves separated within a few years—the fact of which Eric gleaned from numerous evenings spent Facebook stalking Austin after Will went to bed. A few times he even considered sending him a friend request, but what were the odds of him accepting it? People drift apart for a reason, or so said Will once after Eric had received an invitation to his twenty-year high school reunion. Eric had no intention of going, but the vehemence with which Will said it, as if even considering going would be blasphemous, caught him off guard. It was one of those moments that seemed to bring their own relationship into question, the derision in his voice. And so, as far as trying to friend Austin, Eric figured it was better to spare himself the disappointment.

Flicking a piece of lint off his sleeve, Eric asks Ashley how Austin is these days.

"You'd have to ask him. We haven't spoken much." She glances at the patterned carpet. Her tone suggests that there is plenty to be said here but that she doesn't have the energy to go into it. When Eric doesn't comment, she adds, "He works at Hidden Valley Ford. You should go see him."

"I wouldn't want to bother him."

"He wouldn't mind, I'm sure. He has plenty of free time."

"I doubt he'd even remember who I am."

"You were always such a defeatist, Eric." She smiles, though she's only half-joking, and maybe it's the drug draining out of his system, making him feel raw and contentious, but he is annoyed by the jab, the boldness of it, as though they are rekindling an old friendship. He's annoyed by *her*, by the scope of her transformation. It makes him keenly aware of his receding hairline, the slight paunch he's developed since Will tossed him out of the apartment and he no longer has access to the treadmill. The panicky enterprise of aging. At forty-one years old, Eric has come to understand that that's the thing about time: it always seems to favor those least deserving of it.

•

Eric's mother, who had dealt with his father's death by becoming a nuisance at PTA meetings, had arranged the weekly after-school tutoring sessions with Mr. Harmon. Eric suspected the man only agreed to the arrangement to keep her off his back. They met on Friday afternoons, during which time Mr. Harmon would walk him through the problems in the textbook, the two of them sitting close enough behind his desk that Eric could smell his heady musk of deodorant and sweat, a scent that always reminded him, bizarrely, of his father after he arrived home from the Mattress Warehouse he had managed.

"Trigonometry is all about relationships," Mr. Harmon would muse. "It's all interconnected, the angles and lines. Figure out how they correspond to each other, and everything starts to make sense."

Despite his bumbling demeanor, he really was an effective teacher, patient and quippy. He never chastised Eric's inability to interpret the figures on the page as anything other than a secret code devised to his exclusion. Eric might have even come away with a new respect for the material, were it not for the afternoon that, in the middle of a spiel about inverse functions, Mr. Harmon kissed him. It was sloppy and hungry, as though he'd been wanting to do it for some time. His tongue squirmed into his mouth like a rodent looking for shelter, his beard scratching his cheeks, and for an instant Eric wondered, absurdly, if this was some unorthodox teaching strategy. What the hell does anyone know when they're sixteen? The man gripped his thigh, his fingers worming between his legs, and Eric's body tensed as if bracing for a car accident.

Why didn't he push him away? Perhaps because he feared what sort of retaliation embarrassing a teacher might inspire. In eighth grade, he'd had a PE coach who had once made him run twenty laps for pointing out that his zipper was down. "You oughta spend a little more time exercising and little less time staring at men's crotches," he'd taunted Eric from the bleachers as he huffed his way around the basketball court. But there was something else: despite his shock, a part of Eric felt validated, understood. *I see you* Mr. Harmon seemed to be saying with the kiss, or at least this was what Eric wanted to believe, if only to spare himself any indignity. *I know who you are.*

A second later, the man pulled back and slapped a hand over his mouth. The itchy tingle of his beard lingered on Eric's skin. "I shouldn't have done that," he said, his face flushed. "Oh god, Eric, I'm so, so sorry."

For a few minutes, he continued to sputter apologies. Eric assured him that it was okay, even though he understood that one word to Dr. Pell, the principal, and Mr. Harmon would be gone. Except, what if the story got around school? Eric could just imagine what the other kids would say, the names they'd call him, the merciless teasing. And anyway, did he really want him gone?

"You won't tell anyone, will you?" the man pleaded, his fingers forming a cage around his mouth.

"I won't."

"Do you promise, Eric?"

His eyes were glazed with tears. It was hard for Eric not to feel sorry for him. Even harder was trying to figure out what he had done to prompt the kiss, whether he had somehow invited it or if Mr. Harmon had glimpsed in him something that Eric was not yet prepared to acknowledge.

In a voice that he barely recognized as his own, he said, "I promise."

After school, he went to Austin's house. He wanted to tell him what had happened so that he might help him laugh it away. If he could trivialize it, then he wouldn't have to theorize about its meaning. Only, Eric didn't trust Austin to keep it to himself. Instead he said, "Would you ever kiss a teacher?" He was trying to sound offhanded, like the thought had just come to mind.

"What, like on a dare?" Austin said without taking his eyes off *The Real World*.

"I guess, yeah."

"Maybe Mrs. Talbot. She's fine as hell." April Talbot taught sophomore chemistry, a thirty-something redhead with a penchant for the kind of tight pencil skirts and flowy blouses one might associate with softcore porn.

"What about a man?" Eric said.

Now Austin threw him a look. Times like these he seemed to be sizing him up, trying to understand why they were friends. Eric looked at his hand, pretended to examine a cut on his knuckle.

"Why?"

He shrugged. "Just curious."

"Would you?"

"No way, gross."

"Then why ask me?"

Eric didn't say anything. His hope was that Austin might read his face, intuit what had happened. Silence, as they say, speaks volumes. But, as he was beginning to realize, Austin just wasn't the intuitive type.

"Just making conversation," Eric said, returning his eyes to the television, where a group of unreasonably attractive young people were having a staged argument in a well-appointed loft apartment.

"Well, it's weird conversation," Austin grumbled.

"Okay, sorry."

"You're kind of a creeper sometimes, dude."

Eric didn't reply. He could still feel Austin's eyes on him, cold and probing. He focused on the television, refusing to meet his gaze. *You think you know me, but you don't,* one of the cast members was saying. *You think you know everything about the world.*

•

Back at the hotel, Eric scrubs himself raw in the shower, trying to get the funeral home smell out of his pores, a combination of formaldehyde and vanilla potpourri. Snorting another oxy, he heads downstairs to the bar. It's two o'clock and the place is empty, save for a portly couple sitting by the floor-to-ceiling windows, jabbering over a plate of fried calamari. Jazz trickles out of speakers hidden somewhere in the faux tin ceiling. Eric orders a scotch because this seems like the kind of place where you order a scotch, and he thinks about the funeral, all those sharply dressed guests trading stories about Howard Harmon, beloved educator and father. What would they say to know the kind of person he truly was? And what would they think of the fact that Eric never told anyone about the kiss? Would he be viewed as a hero or an enabler?

Certainly Austin would consider him the latter, given his distaste for Mr. Harmon, and in some sense he'd be justified. Probably a good thing, then, that he didn't come to the funeral. What would Eric have even said to him? If his Facebook profile is any indication, they wouldn't have much to talk about. He goes duck hunting, watches golf, follows restaurants like Logan's Steakhouse, even comments on their posts: *oh man those rolls, yummmm lol.* The only thing they share is their high school exploits, and Eric has little desire to relive that part of his life.

"Hating high school is the most boring personality type," Will once told him, another one of his truisms that always came across as more mocking than practical. This was early in their relationship, when they were still getting to know each other and everything felt full of promise. Eric had been griping about his teen years. "You might as well throw on a pair of JNCOs and go work at Hot Topic." He was taken aback by Will's frankness but also charmed. It suggested a self-sufficiency that he wanted to cull for himself.

Which is possibly why now, sitting alone at the bar, the oxy and alcohol effervescing in his veins and the memory of Mr. Harmon's puffy face still fresh in his mind, he is overcome by the need to hear Will's voice, even though he knows the futility of calling him. It's been weeks since Will stopped taking his calls, and so when it goes straight to voicemail Eric is disheartened but not surprised.

The last time they spoke he'd caught Will at work. "This better be life or death," Will hissed upon answering. He worked at an architectural engineering firm that specialized in the kind of glassy modernist high-rises that henchmen are always being tossed from in the movies.

"I have your tennis racket," Eric said.

"Oh, for fuck's sake."

"Do you want me to drop it off or what?"

"Just keep it."

"You don't want it back? It's a nice racket."

"No, Eric. I don't want my goddamn tennis racket back." He sounded more exasperated than angry, a parent arguing with a petulant child, which only amplified Eric's gloominess: how could Will not be as hurt as he was? Why did he get to walk away unscathed while Eric sulked like a teenager?

Cursing himself for not having come up with anything more substantial to say, Eric blurted, "I miss you."

"Here we go."

"I'm serious."

"You're fucked up."

"No, I'm not."

"I can hear it in your voice. You're high."

Eric felt a stab of indignation. Had Will not made his share of mistakes, too? The DUI two years ago? The Superbowl party where Eric caught him in the shadowy corner of the back porch with some frosted-tipped frat boy proxy? Will probably would have countered that those transgressions weren't equivalent to, say, arriving at work to find the police waiting for you and your boss demanding your keys to the schedule II safe back, or having your state pharmacology license revoked, or the threat of jail time. And to that Eric would have pointed out that he has never denied his role in any of his misdeeds. Had he argued when Will demanded he move out? No, he'd gone willingly, assuming that all Will needed was a few days to simmer down. After all, it was hardly their first quarrel. But then a few days became a week, and then two weeks, and then a month, until finally it had become evident that Will no longer had any use for him, excising Eric from his life as cleanly as a benign mole, taking all their mutual friends with him. Not that Eric had much interest in keeping them, but still he wanted to see Will lose *something*, to suffer the way he was, instead of continuing with his life as though nothing had changed.

"What should I do, Will?" he asked. "I'll do anything."

"You should get serious help. Go into a program, something."

"Okay, I will. I swear."

Will made a sound somewhere between a scoff and a chuckle. "You know what the worst thing about you is, Eric? You don't even know when you're lying."

And before Eric could stop himself: "Yes, I do."

Currently, he rests his forehead in his palm. Across the room, the man is laughing at something the woman has said, fat guffaws like shotgun blasts. Downing the last of his drink, Eric lets out a barking laugh of his own, boisterous enough to rouse their attention, their round, fleshy faces brimming with the same contempt seen in mugshots. A part of him almost feels guilty for ridiculing them, these two strangers who are only trying to enjoy their appetizer, and in fact he isn't entirely sure why he's doing it, but that doesn't stop him from laughing in hearty humorless breaths, until his throat his raw and his lungs as sore as if he's just completed a sprint, at which point the bartender tromps over to order him out.

•

The Monday after the incident, Eric spent the whole period waiting for Mr. Harmon to acknowledge him, a look or a nod, but the man seemed to go out of his way not to glance in his direction. Somehow, this was even worse than if he had blurted out to the entire room what had happened. Finally, after class, he asked Eric if he could have a moment of his time. Once the rest of the students had filed out of the room, Mr. Harmon took off his glasses and pinched the bridge of his nose. Without them he looked incomplete, an unfinished caricature. "I just wanted to tell you again how sorry I am about what happened on Friday," he said. "I don't know what came over me. I'm truly embarrassed."

"It's okay," Eric said, only because he didn't know what else to say. He was a kid, the notion of autonomy still hazy.

"You didn't tell anyone, did you?"

"No, sir."

"That's good, that's smart. Because I don't want to think about what might happen if it got out." Reading the confusion on Eric's face, he went on, "I mean, I know you don't want to sit in the office and tell Dr. Pell about it. It's your word against a teacher's, and it's really unfair how often the higherups side with them. Makes me sick, frankly. I worry you'd be doing more damage than good."

Eric studied the man's face, the shadow of his sizable nose, the tiny tuft of fur between his eyebrows. The regretful twist of his mouth, as if he wished he could foster a new world, one in which Eric's word might count.

He went on, "Plus, you've been doing so well lately, seems to me you're likely to finish with an A. And you wouldn't want to jeopardize that, would you?"

"No, sir."

"Glad to hear it," he said, slipping his glasses back on. The effect was astoundingly transformative; he might as well have put on a new face, the way he all at once seemed like a different person. "Really glad, Eric. I knew you were a reasonable guy. Don't forget about the quiz on Thursday."

•

Hidden Valley Ford is a ten-minute drive from the hotel, situated along a busy highway predominated by gas stations and burger joints and payday lenders. It's late fall, and the tree-covered mountains are a riot of reds and golds. In the air is the smoky tartness of autumn, evoking in Eric a simultaneous loneliness and longing for solitude. He pulls into the lot and parks outside the glass-fronted showroom. For a couple moments, he remains in the car, gathering his courage. He watches the dumpy salesmen with their Target ties schmooze with car shoppers. They all have that look of private desperation about them, like they would just as soon blow their brains out than try to upsell another used Mustang.

When he's finally worked up the nerve, he goes into the showroom and asks the receptionist behind the sleek circular desk if Austin is in. She calls for him over the intercom—*"Austin to the showroom, Austin to the showroom."* Watching through the windows as a barrel-chested salesman accosts a young couple looking at a sedan, Eric tries to shake the suspicion that he's walking into a trap. What does it say that in two decades Austin hasn't reached out once? Eric isn't prepared to say, but he supposes it doesn't matter. Loss has a way of making you want to spill your guts: things you've kept private suddenly become a liability.

Eric's mind flashes back to the afternoon that Mr. Harmon warned him about telling anyone what had happened. After school, he and Austin had watched *Pulp Fiction* on HBO. Austin loved violent movies, the gorier the better, possibly because they tended to stoke Eric's squeamishness, which he always seemed to think was good for a laugh. That day, however, Eric was too rattled to offer much of a reaction. It was the blasé tone of Mr. Harmon's voice, as if the whole thing were a mild misunderstanding. Was he crazy for wanting the man to be as affected by it as he was?

"What's wrong with you?" Austin said after a while.

"Nothing."

"You look all sad and shit."

"Got some stuff on my mind."

"What stuff?"

As much as Eric wanted to confide in his friend, he was too scared of what he might be revealing about himself. Scared of what Austin might do with that information.

"Midterms," he lied. "I'm worried about Civics."

"Oh, jeez," Austin said, returning his attention to the movie. "I thought it was something serious, the way you looked."

Why had he been so eager to accept Austin's judgment? Because he needed to believe that he was worth judging at all. It was, he understands now, the same thing that drew him to Will when they met at a spin class three years ago, where he'd been pedaling away contentedly while Eric kept having to peel his sweat-soaked shirt from his frame, his muscles sore and uncooperative: it was Will's self-reliance, the sense that he didn't really need him. At least, not in the desperate, grasping way he needed Will. Unlike Eric, he was admirably disciplined—a single cup of coffee in the mornings after his five-mile run, no red meat or fried foods, maybe a few glasses of wine on Saturdays but never enough to get him drunk. He was usually the one to decide where they would eat or which shows they would watch, not because he was domineering but because Eric, untrusting of his own judgment, was quick to defer.

And so now here is Austin, twenty years later, emerging from behind a hallway on the far side of the room. From the slow, heavy-footed way he moves, like a man who has just been roused out of bed, it's clear how much he's aged. His scalp is visible through his hair, and his gut pooches over his belt. Nevertheless, as he crosses the large room, Eric can see vestiges of his former self: there's the widow's peak, making a heart out of his face, and the ears too, and of course the mangled lip, poorly disguised beneath a salt-and-pepper mustache.

"Eric?" he says, squinting, as if trying to make him out from a great distance.

"Hey, Austin."

He offers Eric a puzzled smile, shakes his hand. His cologne smells cheap and medicinal, like the cough suppressants Eric hocks to his older customers. "Wow, what are you doing here?"

"I was in town, thought I'd stop in."

"How'd you know where I work?"

"Ashley told me. She said I should come by."

"Where'd you see her?"

"Mr. Harmon's funeral."

Austin shoves his hands in his pockets, nods as if confirming something to himself. "I heard about that. What a shame."

"If this is a bad time, I can go."

He seems to consider Eric for a second the same way he used to years ago when Eric said something idiotic, like he's trying to figure out his angle. "No, it's fine. Let's go outside. I could use a smoke, anyway."

Out in the lot, the wind rocks them on their feet, snaps at their jackets. Austin has to hunker down between a pair of F150s to light his cigarette, and it still takes him close to a minute. "They don't like us doing this in front of the customers," he says, examining the smoldering Camel between his knuckles. "They say it's unprofessional."

"Good thing I'm not a customer."

"Well, that sucks, because I could use the commission."

"I can't really afford a car right now."

"I'm fucking with you, Eric. Relax."

Eric tails Austin through the labyrinth of shiny new vehicles, watching his shaggy hair flap in the breeze, recalling the way he used to wind it around his finger while he watched TV. He listens as he gushes about the woman he's been seeing, a bank teller who, he claims, fucks like it's worth a prize. Austin's version of small talk always amounted to him blathering about his own meager exploits, to which Eric would smile and chuckle in all the right places, as he does now, remotely curious as to what Will might say to see him slipping so easily back into a role he was glad to have abandoned.

And perhaps it's the comfort of the role, combined with his desire for Austin to see him as equally hard-nosed, that prompts Eric to fish a pill out of the vial in his pocket and plop it on his tongue in the middle of his soliloquy.

"What do you have there?" Austin says.

"Hurt my back a few months ago. It's for the pain." Then, seeing the way Austin is eying the vial, "You want one?"

"How much?"

"No charge. Help yourself."

He thanks Eric and takes one. "So, how is Ashley?" he asks, downing the tab. "She still with Captain America?"

"The crewcut guy? Yeah, I guess so."

"Figures. How'd she look?"

"Fine. I mean, it was a funeral, you know?"

"Right."

"I had hoped I would see you there."

Austin shrugs. "I wasn't close with the guy, not like you were."

"We weren't close," Eric replies after a beat.

"You did those tutoring sessions, didn't you? Seemed like you knew him a lot better than I did."

Is there a taunting note in his voice, something accusatory? Eric waves smoke out of his face. "I've always wondered why you didn't like him."

"Who, Mr. Harmon? I didn't feel one way or another about him."

"Did he do something to you?"

"Like what?"

"I don't know, something inappropriate."

"What the hell are you talking about, Eric?" Shifting his gaze to the busy road, Austin tosses the half-finished smoke on the ground and lights up once more, his third in ten minutes. "Look, that shit was like a million years ago. I barely remember it. I'm sure as hell not going to get all weepy about a guy I didn't care about in the first place. People die, life goes on."

Eric nods, though there's a hardness to Austin's voice that he recognizes, the insinuation of things long unspoken. He studies his friend's face, the haggard bearing of Austin's eyes and the rogue hairs poking out of the absurd mustache. Of course Austin remembers, how can he not? Men like him and Eric don't know how to jettison the past—how can they when the future looms so ominous? It trails them like a foul odor, not unlike the smell from the funeral home: no matter how much you try, you can never scrub it away completely.

•

When Eric finished the year with an A in trigonometry—the first time he'd received anything over a C in a math class—his mother was predictably ecstatic. To celebrate, she took him to a steakhouse where the servers wore ties and crisply ironed slacks. A massive stone fireplace lent the place a warm elegance. Folks in suits and cocktail dresses bantered merrily over glasses of pinot noir. "I wish your father could be here," she said during their meals, eyes watering. "He'd be so proud." Eric glanced away. If only she'd known—not just about the kiss, but how after it he had stopped turning in assignments altogether, how he had taken to sleeping during class simply because he could. What was

Mr. Harmon going to do about it? Not a thing if he wanted to keep his job. By Eric's own estimation, his actual grade was below a fifty. He wiped at his own moistening eyes, which his mother must have taken as an indication that he'd been moved because she reached across the table and placed her hand over his.

"I'm proud of you, too," she added.

•

By the time Austin announces he needs to get back to the showroom, Eric can feel the itchy craving for another pill, his nerves already beginning to ache, his heart thudding against his sternum. "Thanks for coming by," Austin says. "We should totally get a beer while you're in town."

"Yeah, for sure."

Sheepishly, he motions toward Eric's jacket pocket, where he stowed the oxys. "Any chance I could get one more of those?"

Eric removes the vial, turns it over in his palm. "Here, just take the rest."

"Wow, for real?"

"Sure. Consider it a token of my appreciation."

"For what?"

"For humoring me." No need to tell Austin that he has another vial back at the hotel, and two at his place back in Baltimore. For once, he feels valuable. He's the one who has something to give.

"Safe drive back," Austin says, giving his hand a brisk pump, his grip cold and loose. As he slumps back toward the showroom, Eric understands that this will be the last time they see each other, the last time they speak. Which is okay with him: it's hard to maintain a friendship with someone once they've given you everything they have to offer.

And for people like him and Austin, that isn't much.

Climbing back into his car, Eric starts the engine but doesn't leave the dealership yet. He watches the leaves skittering across the lot in the breeze, and he thinks about Mr. Harmon, the dry prickly feel of his lips, his hand grasping his thigh. "You're all capable of great things," he'd told the room on the last day of classes, though Eric got the sense that he was addressing him in particular, and somehow even then he knew it was the first of many promises that would never deliver.

So now, slipping his phone out of his pocket, he dials Will's number. When it goes to voicemail, he's actually relieved. He has a story to share, and he doesn't want to be interrupted.

Raise Your Fists

From the windowless dressing room behind the stage, Frank could hear the crowd of mohawked punks chanting his name—"*Frank*-ie! *Frank*-ie! *Frank*-ie!" There was a time when that sound would have made him feel like royalty, but tonight he was content to keep them waiting. The opening band had finished its set over forty-five minutes earlier and his backing band was waiting for him on-stage. The club manager had already been in twice to ask, politely but not without frustration, what the holdup was. But Frank had never let himself be browbeaten by club managers, and he wasn't about to start now. After nearly forty years of touring and three gold albums, hadn't he earned the right to take his goddamn time?

They were in Richmond, another divey stop on his farewell tour. It was the kind of place he would have played early in his career, before he went solo, which was how he had pitched the tour to the label, as a throwback to his younger days. Graffiti covered the brick walls, crude caricatures and tagger names and a smattering of anarchy signs. The bar was plastered over with ancient band stickers, the bathroom practically third world. Wearing only a pair of frayed jeans—his customary stage attire—he was on the concrete floor in child's pose, his knees bent beneath his tawny chest and his arms stretched out before him. It was one of the few yoga poses taught to him by his personal assistant Naomi who, ever since his diagnosis six months prior, had diligently sought out every memory-sustaining measure she could find, including the kale smoothies she insisted he choke down daily, as evidenced by the globby green remnants in the blender on the wet bar across the room. Yoga, she claimed, increased gray matter density. And while Frank wasn't entirely certain what this meant, and he suspected that she wasn't either, he couldn't deny that the stretches loosened him up before a performance. And at sixty-five years old—not quite elderly but still decades older than most of the acts dominating the scene these days—he was finding it increasingly difficult to stay limber.

Having made a career of hard living, Frank had always imagined he would saunter into old age like the guest of honor at a party, elegantly poised and ready to be received. He had never anticipated the indignity of, say, compression socks or stool softeners or, sure, incontinence, all of which flew in the face of the fuck-it-all aesthetic he'd cultivated. Or, much worse, the gradual deterioration of his brain, the memory lapses and the disorientation, as though time had begun to warp around him like liquid. Things that wouldn't faze a child had started to perplex him—using a calculator, for instance, or counting out change. Names and dates vanished from his mind like embers blinking out of the air. More than once he'd forgotten to finish putting on clothes before leaving the house. Lewy body dementia, the neurologist had called it, small protein deposits in the cerebral cortex. "They're like little roadblocks," he'd explained. "They slow down the signals moving between neurons."

"How do I get rid of them?" Frank had asked.

"No cure, I'm afraid." The doc had spoken with the faux solemnity of a boss terminating an employee he barely knew. "But you can slow the process. Probably going to have to make some major lifestyle changes. Diet and exercise, that's your best course of action."

For a few moments, Frank had sat quietly, drumming his fingers on the armrests of the padded chair. Despite the severity of the diagnosis, he'd felt a minor wave of relief: now that he knew what he was dealing with, he could concoct a plan. And the first step of that plan was figuring out what he would tell Pete. Or, if he should tell him at all. It had been almost a decade since his son had spoken to him, and Frank had no reason to suspect that his feelings had changed. Then again, every artist understood that opportunities announce themselves in the most peculiar of ways: maybe this was a chance to make amends. Above all, Frank needed to know that he had someone in his corner other than Naomi who, loyal though she may have been, was no caretaker. Not that Pete was either, but they were blood—surely that had to count for something.

The next day Frank had called Pete. His wife Sheila answered his phone. "He's driving," she grumbled when Frank asked to speak with his son. "What's this concerning?"

"I'd rather talk to him about it, Sheila."

"Like I said, he's driving."

"Goddammit, does he have two hands or not?"

Groaning, she handed over the phone to her husband.

"Going to be coming through Richmond next month," he told Pete. "I'd really like to see you."

"It's not the best time right now," Pete replied flatly.

"I'm not talking about now. I'm talking about a month from now."

"I just don't think it's a great idea, Frank."

"Look, it's important, okay? Half an hour, that's all I'm asking."

"You can't just do it over the phone?"

Why Frank was so caught off-guard by his son's standoffishness, he didn't know—perhaps because he'd assumed that eight years would have been enough time for his bitterness to abate. People, in his experience, weren't worth the energy that grudges demanded; better to channel that energy into creative pursuits, but then Pete was hardly the creative type. He could have told him about his meeting with the doctor, about the MRI images of his brain studded with tiny white spots like stars in a bleary sky. He could have told him about how, just the previous week, he'd zoned out in Target—that was how the literature packet that the doc had given him referred to it, "zoning out"—for several minutes, during which time he'd gotten separated from Naomi. Too overwhelmed by his own paranoia to find a way out of the labyrinth of aisles, he had cursed uncontrollably at the teenaged employee offering to help and had nearly been thrown out, until Naomi reappeared and ushered him away.

However, this all seemed like a lot to drop in his son's lap, especially after so many years of estrangement. Instead, he said, "I think face-to-face is better."

Pete was silent for a couple seconds. "Are you dying or something?"

"Don't be stupid, I'm never going to die."

"You say that like it's a threat."

•

Currently, as Frank moved into upward-facing dog, Naomi slipped into the room, the volume of the crowd momentarily spiking before she shut the door behind her. She'd been out at the bar trying to smooth things over with the manager, a task she'd undertaken several times already on the tour when Frank, even despite the three bumps of coke he ritualistically snorted before each show, just hadn't had the energy to face his fans. "Dude's getting impatient," she warned. "Crowd, too."

"They'll survive."

“They paid money to see you, Frank. You can’t keep doing this.”

“Doing what?”

“Being a diva.”

“I’m stretching.”

“You’re stalling.”

Frank sat up on his knees, his joints popping like twigs. A less seasoned performer might have been put off by his assistant snapping orders at him, but after seven years he had come to appreciate Naomi’s directness, her ability to counterbalance his own notoriously awful decision-making. And anyway, she was right, he *was* stalling. But how were you supposed to explain to a thirty-five-year-old the all-consuming fear of knowing that your mind was no longer trustworthy? What if his brain glitched while he was on stage? The last thing he wanted was for his fans to remember him as some senile jackass bumbling around like a crazy person, especially given that most of them would be recording the show on their phones. The whole point of retirement was to stop before he went out as a joke.

Naomi hunkered down so she could meet him head-on. With her shaved head and finger-thick septum ring, she could have passed for a man, were it not for her skirt and ripped up fishnets. “It’ll be okay,” she said, a near-whisper, placing a hand on Frank’s bare shoulder. “I promise.” Yet, as reassuring as she sounded, there was no mistaking the doubt in her eyes, searching his face as if mentally mapping each peak and cleft. Like this was the last time she would ever see him.

All the same, Frank didn’t want his fans to remember him as someone who screwed them out of a hundred dollars either. Plus, hadn’t he always believed that the stage was the ideal place to confront one’s mortality? A man should die proudly when it is no longer possible to live proudly, or so said Friedrich Nietzsche—Frank had read it on a beer coaster somewhere—and at this point in his life, what more was there to want besides a proud death? And so finally he came to his feet and, after Naomi had straightened the spikes of his fuchsia-colored hair, he followed her out into the narrow corridor leading to the stage, trying to suppress the sensation that he was being led to his execution.

•

If you were tuned into the East Coast punk scene in the late eighties, you knew Frank Pagnarelli, better known by his stage name Frankie Fury. Maybe you'd listened to his work with Blast Radius and Vomitorium and then his solo work, which included twelve studio albums and a slew of live releases. You might have even caught one of his shows, which one *Rolling Stone* journalist described as "a raucous celebration of the id." The accompanying photo depicted him standing before a rack of S & M gear, whips and chains and the like, a nod to his practice of self-mutilation during performances, like when he would carve words into his chest with a boxcutter, *fight* or *riot* or something equally rousing (he'd toned down the cutting ever since the 2007 infection that had landed him in the ICU, though his chest still bore a tapestry of scars). Or like the time in Tulsa eight years ago when he drank his own urine out of a stiletto, which cost him five hundred dollars for violating a lewdness ordinance, as well as any chance to ever play the Tulsa Performing Arts Center again.

By the time Pete called him days later, a few networks and blogs had already picked up the story. A cellphone video had appeared online, and there was even a gif circulating on social media. "Do you not realize how this affects the people around you?" he'd snapped. Over the years, Pete's indignation over his father's antics had only intensified as the stunts had grown more outlandish, and while Frank was disheartened to hear the ire in his son's voice, he was hardly surprised. "You don't hear what the other kids at school say to Matt. They're ruthless."

"Kids say a lot of things," Frank argued. The bullying, he suspected, had less to do with the incident and more to do with the fact that Matt was a mousy kid with a peanut allergy and an asthma inhaler he wielded like a talisman. "Maybe you should teach him to throw a punch. He's practically a teenager anyway."

"He's eleven, Frank. And that's not the point. I have an image to uphold. I can't have my clients associating me with that kind of stuff."

"Your *image*? What are you, a fucking politician now?" Pete did something with real estate, though Frank could never recall his title.

Pete sighed. "I've had all I can handle. I have a family to look after."

"Meaning what?"

"Meaning that I think a clean break is best. For all of us."

Frank didn't know what to say. He had always believed his son's lifelong embarrassment to be normal, just as he'd been mortified by his own dad's fondness for limericks or his encyclopedic knowledge of Civil War generals. Parents embarrassed their kids, that was gospel. Of course, most parents didn't make a living by debasing themselves for roomfuls of disgruntled punks, but what else was Frank supposed to do, go work in a cubicle? You did what you were good at, everybody knew that, and flirting with the boundaries of good taste was the only thing that had ever come naturally to him.

"Pete," he said, gentler, "this is my job. This is what I get paid to do."

"No one ever pushed you into it," he replied. "It's still your choice. It always has been." Then he hung up.

•

By the time Frank emerged from the back of the club, the crowd, most of them twenty-somethings with the occasional paunchy middle-ager mixed in, was poised to riot, chucking bottles and pieces of trash toward the stage. Once he positioned himself behind the mic, however, spreading his arms crucifixion-style, all was forgiven, a rowdy chorus of cheers erupting as he cued the band into "Raise Your Fists," the most iconic tune off his first solo album. Bodies began to churn, colliding into each other like atoms generating heat, the familiar tang of sweat and beer and smoke rising up thick as steam.

"They're coming for your body," he barked into the mic, *"they're coming for your voice, they're coming for your freedom, and you don't have a choice!"*

And yet, even as he prowled the stage with the galvanizing authority of a televangelist, inches from the outstretched fingers of all those baby-faced hipsters, he couldn't keep his mind from drifting back to his conversation with Pete earlier that day. They had met up at a Starbucks not far from the club, Pete's suggestion, in a posh shopping center predominated by health food stores and wine shops. Frank had arrived ten minutes early and, after ordering his tea—no caffeine, Naomi's orders—had taken a seat by the window. Looking out at the swank cars glinting in the afternoon sun, he'd thought about his first few years of fatherhood. Pete's mother had been a temp at the first label Frank had signed to, which had gone belly-up only a few years later, not unlike the marriage itself, whose dissolution had come as a relief to both parties. Not to Pete, though, who had been five at the time. Would he have been more understanding if Frank hadn't spent the bulk of his childhood on the road, playing shows and giving interviews, weathering the occasional detox stint, which had always left him feeling more depressed than when he started? He was probably better off not knowing.

Fifteen minutes later, a white Acura swung into the parking lot, and out climbed Pete, lumbering toward the door with his phone clamped to his ear. Unlike Frank, who bordered on skeletal, Pete had always been husky, though in the intervening years he appeared to have packed on an additional fifty pounds or so, his gut dripping over his belt, his nearly bald head as large and rounded as an engorged toe. Dressed in a polo shirt, khakis, and loafers, he was a startling contrast to Frank, in his grungy denim vest and engineer boots. In fact, he looked every bit the corporate stooge that Frank's music was intended to lampoon.

Still, he was there, wasn't he? Yes, Frank had to remind himself as his son waddled into the coffee shop and then made his way toward him, the kid had come to meet, which meant that maybe he was open to some form of reconciliation. Except, when Frank went in for a fatherly clap on the back, Pete stuck out his hand for a shake, halting him. His grip was soft, noncommittal. After he had ordered his mocha frappuccino and returned to the small table, having refused Frank's offer to reimburse him for the drink, the two of them sat in silence, unsure of sure how to proceed. "So, I'm here," he said when the quiet had become too uncomfortable.

"I appreciate it," Frank replied. "It's good to see you."

"What do you want?"

Frank threw an arm over the back of his chair, trying to appear unfazed by his son's aloofness. "How are Sheila and Matt?"

"They're fine."

"What is Matt now, like seventeen?"

"Nineteen."

"Wow, shit, okay. So, he's in college, right?"

"We're not doing this."

"Doing what?"

"I don't want to play catch-up with you, Frank." Pete crossed his chubby arms. "Just tell me what you want."

Frank looked around the shop at the students clacking away on laptops, the gaggle of young moms in the back-corner bantering over their macchiatos and casting the occasional glance in his direction—it's not every day you see a grown man with hair like a sea anemone—and then back at his son. The buttoned-down schlub he had become. Even as a teenager, Pete had been straightlaced, shunning parties and concerts in favor of study sessions and Future Business Leaders of America meetings. The kind of kid who straddled the boundary between overachiever and toady. Frank recalled the time, during one of his infrequent visits to town when Pete was sixteen, he'd advised him against becoming an adult too soon. They'd been at some Italian joint, Pete poking sullenly at his pasta pomodoro. "You should try to have more fun, enjoy yourself," Frank had said, mainly just to have something to say. "There's plenty of time to be average."

"I think you and I have very different ideas of fun," Pete had mumbled into his meal.

"What the hell's that supposed to mean?"

"It means I'm not like you. I actually take things seriously. Sorry if you can't get your head around that."

"Come on, I take plenty of things seriously." Frank's tone was playful, like they were just razzing each other. "I'm serious as a heart attack, baby. I'm the most serious son of a bitch in this place."

But Pete wasn't the razzing type, or so he was learning, and when the boy finally cut his eyes at him, Frank's smirk had faltered. "Just not about the things that matter," he'd said.

So now, seated across from his son in Starbucks, Frank pressed on, "Alright, well, I'm sick, I guess you could say."

"Sick how?"

Frank filled him in on what the doctor had said. He told him about the memory problems and the MRI images, though he stopped short of divulging the Target story. The last thing he wanted was to present himself as unhinged.

"Jeez, I'm sorry to hear that, truly," Pete said when he was finished, and to Frank's surprise he sounded sincere. "How long until—well, you know?"

"Could be months, could be years, the doc says. He thinks I should start doing puzzles, sudoku and shit."

"Might not be a bad idea."

"Fuck that. I'm not going to spend the little time I have left doing math."

"Maybe wordsearches then?"

"Or maybe a bullet in my skull?"

"Jesus Christ, I'm just trying to be helpful here."

"I want to give you power of attorney."

Pete looked as if someone had just blown an air horn in his ear. "What the hell are you talking about?"

"Look, I have no idea what's going to happen to me. I need someone who can steer me in the right direction. Someone I can trust."

"You want me to take care of you?"

Frank shook his head. "I want you to decide what's best when the time comes."

Sitting back in his seat like he'd just received devastating news, Pete looked out toward the parking lot. Frank watched his face the way you might watch a sky for rain. Everything he'd read about the condition had stressed the importance of having somebody standing by to act on your behalf, a surrogate. Ideally, Frank would have given the job to Naomi, but that was a lot to ask of someone who probably had plans for her own life beyond handling his laundry and securing acid for him. But then, who else was there other than his boy? For all his years spent consorting with industry figures and musicians, there were very few folks he could turn to. His hope had been that the news of his father's illness would be enough for Pete to set aside his resentment and rise to the occasion. A long shot for sure, but as Naomi had contended, when it came to matters of life and death, what choice did you have other than to trust people to make the right decisions?

Which was why Frank was stunned when, after nearly a minute, Pete responded, "No."

"No?"

"I'm sorry you're sick, Frank, I really am. But this isn't my problem anymore."

"Pete, I'm just asking you to think about it—"

"You're asking me to play babysitter to a man I haven't seen in ten years."

"Eight."

"Whatever. My point is that you can't just show up out of the blue and expect things to suddenly be normal, like the past never happened." A swig of his drink and then, wiping the whipped cream off his lip, "I mean, I hardly even know you."

"Stop being dramatic," Frank fired back, though it was true that their relationship had never really developed beyond a passive acquaintanceship. By the time Pete's teens rolled around the novelty of his father's notoriety had worn away and he'd started to regard Frank's semi-annual visits, which usually involved dinner at a chain restaurant or a trip to the mall, as punitive, something he was required to endure. Maybe he blamed Frank for the way things had ended between him and his mother. (Even Frank, whose prurient appetites had run deep back then, had to acknowledge he hadn't been much of a husband.) Or maybe he resented feeling like another obligation to which his father had to tend, who knew. In any case, a barrier had been erected, and no matter what Frank tried—invitations to shows, cash-stuffed envelopes slipped to the boy like secret documents between spies—he just couldn't penetrate it. In the years preceding the Tulsa incident, he and Pete had spoken only a handful of times, holidays and birthdays mostly, and never for more than a few minutes at a stretch.

Which was what had made Pete's decision to cut him out of his life so confounding. What did he think he was escaping? It wasn't like he'd be anymore insulated from the blowback of his father's stunts. Like it or not, he would always be Frankie Fury's son.

"I asked you on the phone if you were dying," Pete said. "You could have just told me then."

"I'm not *dying*, for god's sake."

"You know what I mean."

"What do you want me to say, Pete? I wanted to see you."

"Why?"

"Wasn't aware I needed a reason to see my own damn kid."

"A guy like you always has a reason, Frank."

•

It wasn't until the band had stopped playing that Frank was suddenly jolted out of the memory, and he realized with a stab of horror that he had zoned out again. Looking out at the sea of pierced, sweaty faces, all of them focused on him, he wondered how long he'd been standing there wordlessly. Long enough for him to feel like he'd been startled out of a deep sleep and, consequently, to have lost track of where they were in the song. The lyrics, he could see them in the back of his mind like half-erased words on a chalkboard, but for some reason he couldn't access them. The audience watched him with the anticipation of a congregation waiting for the remainder of the sermon, phones upraised to record, and Frank felt the paranoia blooming in his gut again, sharp and icy. Hadn't the neurologist cautioned him about something like this happening? Hadn't he even tried to talk Frank out of the tour all together, stressing his need for a calm, familiar environment going forward? "This is serious business, Frank," the man had said, irritated, as if he was lecturing a disobedient teenager. "You need to establish routines. The last thing you need is more unpredictability."

But Frank, who had never put much stock in doctors anyway, had waved him off. "I've been doing this longer than you've been alive. I know exactly what to expect."

•

When Pete was young, even their most contentious visits had ended with Frank nursing a secret hope that he would beg him to stick around. *You don't have to go*, he'd say. *You can stay here with me.* Would Frank have done it? He wasn't prepared to say—some men just weren't engineered to remain in one place—but he wanted his kid to want him around, that was the point. But Pete never did, not once, and so the visits had always concluded the same way: with Frank giving him a pat on the shoulder and sending him on his way, and then returning to his hotel to get blitzed enough to forget it had ever happened. It wasn't until years later, after Pete had gotten married and had a kid of his own and settled into a life that to Frank had always seemed like a form of surrender, that he would recognize the truth: conformity was the only form of rebellion that had ever been available to him. It made sense in a backwards sort of way. When your father was an antiestablishment icon, how else were you supposed to carve your own path other than embracing mediocrity?

Regardless, this didn't make it any less cutting to know that his son had crafted his own life in opposition to his. Now, as Frank followed Pete out of the Starbucks and across the parking lot to his Acura, he imagined what they must have looked like to anyone looking on, the stuffy blueblood in pleated pants and the tattooed geezer with the dyed hair. Other than their similarly squarish jawlines and long aquiline noses, would anybody have even suspected them of being father and son?

"You should come to the show tonight," he said as they reached the car. "I know it's not really your thing, but you could hang out backstage, have a drink. You could tell me about Matt."

"Thanks, but Sheila and I are going to the movies."

"What are you going to see?"

Standing at the car door with the key fob in his hand, Pete sighed as if the question was too exhausting to answer. He opened the door and stuffed himself in, grunting with the effort. "Take care of yourself, Frank. We'll be praying for you."

•

How long did Frank stand there staring out at the audience, motionless, his heart threatening to hammer its way out of his chest? Seconds maybe, though it might as well have been years. He wanted, for reasons he couldn't understand, to tell them everything—about watching his son swing out of the parking lot and speed away, and about the MRIs, the protein clumps in his brain, the increasingly frequent fugue states. He wanted to explain about the yoga and the goddamn smoothies. The agonizing process of losing yourself piece by piece. He wanted to tell them that if the past year had taught him anything, it was that the things that matter most are the ones you lose first.

And he might have, too, had his attention not been snagged by the figure off to the left of the stage—a head, hairless and rounded, hovering near the fire exit. An anomaly in the field of spiky hairstyles. Frank inched toward the edge of the stage, straining to see through the lights and the smoke and his own mental fog. If it was Pete, he decided right then, he would tell him about the Target incident. Yes, he would tell him how scared and alone he felt. Not because Frank wanted a surrogate but because he needed to hear himself say it to someone, and it seemed imperative that it be Pete. He would even offer an apology, though for what he had no clue—he just wanted to have something to offer his son.

It was only a moment after he realized that the head belonged to Naomi, who was watching him the way you might observe a tragedy unfold, that the first bottle struck him. It glanced off his shoulder, prompting a round of cheers from the crowd. The next one came within inches of his head, shattering against the kickdrum. Naomi's face went taut with panic. Then came a can clattering against his chest, and then another clanging off a cymbal, then another bottle and more cans and crumpled cigarette packs and a few lit butts, a barrage of garbage. Clearly, the audience had had enough of his stalling. Not that Frank could really blame them, which was why he stayed where he was, even as the band ditched their instruments and fled the stage, and even as Naomi battled her way toward him through the crush of bodies, presumably with the intention of dragging him out of harm's way, he held his ground.

Whether the lyrics' reappearance in his mind was inspired by the uproar, Frank didn't know. All he knew was that suddenly they were just *there*, a light flicking on in the darkness. It was the chorus of the song, which he'd written over forty years earlier when Pete was still a baby: *It's time to raise your fists! It's time to resist!* It was meant as an indictment of the capitalist status quo, or so he'd claimed to any number of rock journalists, though the truth was that, like most of his music, it had just sounded angsty and adversarial enough to rile up a crowd. That was all he'd ever wanted really, to get a rise out of people with his music. To challenge them. If only Pete had understood that, but as Frank was discovering, sometimes even understanding was too much to ask.

So now, spreading his arms to welcome the onslaught, Frank once more belted the words into the mic, knowing that one day they would be gone for good. Like everything else, they would vanish from his memory and there would be no way to retrieve them, and who would be there to rescue him? Only, that didn't matter now. What mattered was that he kept singing through the booing and the cursing, kept chanting the lyrics over and over like an incantation, until the barrage threatened to become an all-out riot, at which point Naomi burst onto the stage and wrapped her arms around him, a human shield, the two of them toppling over onto the garbage-strewn stage. Frank's head bounced off the ancient carpet. He gazed up at the ceiling, the exposed beams and blinding stage lights. "You're okay," Naomi said, her mouth next to his ear, the trash raining down around them. "I've got you."

Solve

1. Rick is traveling east on his motorcycle at 45 miles per hour. Wind speed is 6 miles per hour. He left Sierra's 5 minutes ago at 3:05 PM. They spent the past hour arguing after Sierra, having borrowed Rick's computer to complete a job application for the Foot Locker, stumbled upon a string of Facebook messages he had sent to other women over the past several months. Rick maintained that these exchanges were harmless, perhaps a bit too flirtatious at times, okay fine, like the one to the girl he met at the tattoo expo in which he mentioned off-handedly that he liked women with tongue studs. Still, it would be a reach to call that *sexual*—although that didn't matter to Sierra, whose previous boyfriend had been notoriously unfaithful; more than once she's rehashed for Rick the saga of her grisly gonorrhea bout, as though she believes this gives her some sort of street cred. She demanded that Rick delete his account immediately, or else she would contact each woman's place of employment to notify them that they were paying bona fide whores. Rick, no stranger to Sierra's idle threats, told her to go ahead and contact them, he didn't give a flying fuck, and

then he stormed out of the apartment. Where he is headed now, he does not know, nor does he care—away from Sierra, that's all that matters. After 6 miles and minimal traffic, Rick accelerates to 66 miles per hour. He weighs 225 pounds, much of it flab, though he likes to imagine it is muscle from his years as a varsity wrestler, a period of time that now seems both ancient history and disturbingly recent, like a vivid dream that lingers even after he's awoken. And if there is anything that 41 years on the planet has taught him, it is that this is how it is with most of the things he wants: they only *seem* real, but look a little closer and you find that there was nothing worth chasing in the first place. The motorcycle weighs 655 pounds. The friction coefficient between the tires and the road is 0.7.

> Q: What time will Rick accidentally run the red light and collide with the front end of the RAV4, and how far (in feet) will his body be thrown?

2. Ashley's resting heart rate is 70 beats per minute. Or at least that's the case when Dylan isn't shrieking in the backseat, as he is now. He wanted Sour Patch Kids from Kroger, but Ashley insisted it would ruin his dinner. The truth is that she would have gladly gotten him something to shut him up if she could have afforded it. But as Wayne is constantly reminding her, they aren't rolling in cash these days, not since the stump removal company for whom he worked since 2017 folded during the pandemic, leaving him jobless. She offers Dylan a packet of raisins, but he smacks them out of her hand. They scatter across the floorboard, at which point her heart rate spikes to 120 beats per minute. Just one more thing she'll have to clean out of the backseat this weekend, along with the spilled juice and the stray Cheez-Its, the splotches of unidentifiable fluids on the door

panel and floorboards that leave her fingers tacky, all while Wayne sprawls on the sofa watching *Better Call Saul*, too despondent over his run of bad luck to lift a finger. *This is what you wanted*, he always whines on the rare occasions that she complains about the demands of motherhood. The way he says it always makes it sound as if her frazzled patience is somehow an affront to him. No point in telling him about the number of times she's sat in the RAV and wept while Dylan dozed in the backseat, or how she sometimes wonders if they should have gone to the women's clinic in Charleston like they discussed that one time, or the ghastly fantasies she's had of abandoning him at a fire station. She supposes it's not Wayne's fault, not totally; as her mother used to say, there is only so much that men can understand at any one time. The light turns green and Ashley inches forward onto the highway. She spots the motorcycle out of the corner of her eye only a fraction of a second before it plows into the front left corner of the RAV, catapulting the driver over the hood. He barrels onto the hardtop, rolling a few times, arms flailing like one of those inflatable figures outside car dealerships, until he comes to a stop, face-down, several yards from the vehicle. Her heart rate accelerates to 174 beats per minute.

> Q: What is the difference in beats per minute between Ashley's current heart rate and the maximum heart rate of a twenty-four-year-old woman?

3. There are roughly 5.2×10^6 cubic centimeters of blood in Rick's body. Having forgone a helmet (not a requirement in South Carolina), his head is hemorrhaging 20 cubic centimeters of blood per second which, even despite his fractured skull and collar bone and his splintered pelvis, imbues him with a flighty, weightless sensation that drifts through his body like a breeze. Actually,

it isn't all that dissimilar from when he and Sierra went skydiving last year. It had been her idea, the two of them strapped to the fronts of their respective instructors like oversized babies being toted around by their parents. He hadn't been prepared for the serenity of freefalling, the way the tension drained from his limbs, easy as vapor, as he plummeted toward the earth. When his instructor had told him to pull the chute, he'd resisted. *Pull the goddamn cord!* the man barked in his ear, but still Rick refused. Finally, the instructor pulled his own cord, deploying the red and white parachute, but already the experience had broken something open in Rick, something that even then he knew he would never be able to stitch back together. And he wasn't sure he wanted to. No, what he wanted in that moment was to keep falling for as long as possible, even if it meant slamming into the ground and turning into jelly. Upon landing, he found Sierra, still strapped to her harried-looking instructor, in hysterics, the fall having been far more frightening than she'd anticipated. (And hadn't Rick tried to warn her about this, how someone for whom even a Ferris wheel ride is an exercise in dizziness didn't have the stomach to jump out of an airplane?) Once the man had freed her from the tandem harness, she'd dashed to Rick and buried her face in his chest. *I didn't know it would be like that!* she'd sobbed. He comforted her the best he could, stroking her sweaty auburn hair and rubbing her back. *Neither did* I, he'd wanted to say, but he'd kept quiet because it wouldn't have meant the same thing. The average adult can tolerate a 30%-40% loss of blood before the onset of shock.

Q: If Rick's blood loss remains steady, how many milliliters of transfused blood will he require to prevent cardiac arrest?

- **A.** 60
- **B.** 600
- **C.** 6,000
- **D.** Cardiac arrest is inevitable

4. The ambulance skids to a stop on the graveled shoulder, scattering the crowd of onlookers that has emerged from the nearby fast-food joints and auto parts stores to gawk at the motionless body. The man—heavyset, jowly, face coated with scruff—reminds Ashley of Wayne, the thought of which sends a surge of bile into her throat. No helmet—*oh god*. She is standing a few yards from the body, Dylan clinging to her neck, both of them puffy-eyed from crying. The motorcycle lies in the road a few yards away like road-kill, front wheel and handlebars grotesquely bent. As the EMTs scurry around the scene, checking the man's eyes with a penlight and gingerly transferring him to a gurney, a police officer with a grape-sized mole on his nostril takes Ashley's statement, assailing her with questions: *How fast were you going? When did you notice the motorcycle? How quickly did you apply the brake?* Dylan squirms in her arms, desperate to go home, and Ashley has to keep adjusting him on her hip. Christ, what if there's a trial? How will they afford an attorney? And if they lose, what then? It wasn't her fault, surely any of the witnesses would attest to this, but people have gone to prison for far less. You hear about it all the time, some poor sap locked up for decades over something that barely constitutes an offense. As the EMTs are loading the body (no, not *body—person*, loading the *person*) into the back of the ambulance, Ashley shoulders past the officer, dashing around the gritty smear of maroon on the road toward the vehicle. *Is he okay*? she says. *Is he alive?* The EMTs don't answer, they are too busy fitting the traction collar around the man's thick neck and monitoring his pulse, but she can see the rise and fall of his chest, and she can make out a choked moan escaping his throat like the sound of the ancient pipes underneath her modular house which are always giving them problems, despite Wayne's attempts to repair them. The man is alive, and that's at least something, though it's anyone's guess what might happen between now and the time he reaches the hospital. The ambulance weighs

10,000 pounds. It pulls onto the road at an initial rate of 3 feet per second and then accelerates to 88 feet per second.

> **Q:** What is the ambulance's rate of acceleration after 10 seconds? Bonus: What is its relative speed to that of Ashley if she is walking in the opposite direction, back toward the bored-looking officer with a snotty-nosed toddler in her aching arms, at a rate of 4.5 feet per second, though to her it's like battling her way through waist-high surf, each step requiring more effort than the last, all the while feeling as though she might lose her footing at any moment and be swept out to sea?

5. Rick isn't sure how he ended up in the ambulance. One second he was coasting down the highway, the August sun on his face and neck, the next he was strapped to the gurney. Vaguely, he recalls crashing into the car—an SUV, he remembers that—but only as a series of disjointed images: there's the bike, then the car, then the road. In some remote channel of his consciousness, he's aware that he is severely injured, and it occurs to him that he might die, might *already* be dead—the thought of which isn't as terrifying as he might have predicted. In fact, it's curiously comforting: no more worrying over his bank account, his weight, his future, no more battling with the ill-tempered forklift at Home Depot, which he's been driving for the past two years and would probably otherwise drive until the day he retires. No more wondering when his fortune will change, when he'll finally get his moment, find a better career, take the bike out to Sedona, maybe get back into playing guitar, write and record some songs, an album, win the Powerball, clock the son of a bitch mayor, whatever. No more Sierra either, which is sad, though on some level he's always known that they wouldn't last. Whether she realizes it or not, they've simply been biding their time, waiting for something better to come along. Or at least *he* has. And now that he's come face-to-face with his own mortality, he feels bad about that. He does. He could have been better to her; he should have eased off the fooling around, been more honest, less of a hothead. He could have done Christmas with her in Asheville last year like she pleaded, instead of insisting that they stay in town, hit up the few bars that would be open on the 25th. What was the point? Why not grant her that one simple request? Because something in him longs to harm the people closest to him. To throw around what little power he has. He's never understood it, but there it is. He's a jerk, a bastard. He's shit. He's lower than shit. If he really is dying, then he deserves it. Only, he doesn't *want* to die. Even if it means freedom, he's not ready—no, God, not now, not when he's started to see the world for what it is, to see beyond the veil of the self that clouds everything, beyond what he *believes* he knows into what he *actually* knows and holy shit is it something, so much light, so much to behold when you step outside your own body—how has he lived his whole life not knowing how small he is, how irrelevant, and how wonderful it is to recognize that there is nothing separating you from whatever lies beyond the physical? Why is it that *trying* to exist achieves the exact opposite outcome? How have all his questions about life, about himself, always been the wrong ones? On average, the human brain contains 86 billion neurons. Rick's neurons are dying off at a rate of 2 million per minute.

> Q: How long will it take Rick, currently in the throes of a hallucination brought about by trauma to the hippocampus and temporoparietal junction, though blessedly free from any pain, to lose all his neurons? Bonus: if Rick's rate of neuron loss equates to 4 years of brain aging per hour, what age will his brain approximate once all the neurons have died?

6. After the ambulance has sped away, and after Ashley has tearfully phoned Wayne about the accident, only to be subjected to a ten-minute rant about what this might do to their insurance, she straps Dylan back into his car seat. He is tired and scared and hungry. To pacify him, she offers a small bag of Cheetos, dinner be damned, but he swats at her hands as she fumbles with the buckle, wailing at the top of his lungs. Unable to stop herself, Ashley shrieks at him to shut the fuck up. For a second, he regards her with silent terror as if she's just struck him. Ashley, too, is silent, mortified by what has just escaped her mouth. When his wailing recommences, it's even more shrill. Desperately, she walks back the outburst, *Oh baby, I'm so sorry, Mommy didn't mean it, please please please, Mommy is so sorry*, trying to wrap her arms around him, but he pushes her away, *No, Mommy, no!* Too spent to cry anymore, she slumps against the vehicle's open door. Her body aches; it feels cumbersome and alien. She wonders what Wayne would do if he were here but then pushes the idea aside, because he *isn't* here, and truth be told she's glad. For all of his blustering, Wayne doesn't have an eye for *solutions*. Sure, he can fix a busted dryer or change out a car battery, but he doesn't know how to make his life, *their* lives, any better. Which is not to say that Ashley does, but she tries, goddammit. Only, she's tired of trying, tired of her efforts continually failing. For example: the raisins she offered to Dylan, which she now spies constellated across the dirty floorboard beneath his feet. Should she have just gotten him the candy, if only to spare herself the headache? When is it okay to do what is easy over what is right? She doesn't know. Nor does she know what compels her to gather them up and start popping them into her mouth one by one. Grains of sand from this past weekend's beach excursion stick to them, grinding between her teeth. It's enough to make her queasy as she swallows. (If it were Dylan, she would knock them out of his hand.) But she can't help herself, not until she notices that Dylan has

stopped bawling and is watching her with a curious grin, as if he thinks it's a performance, and he says *Why you eat that, Mommy?* to which Ashley, her self-disgust overruled by a wave of affection for her only child, flashes him a smile, the chewed-up raisins mashed against her teeth, which elicits a giggle, and it's the most amazing sound she's ever heard, better than being told she was going to be a mother, it makes her almost woozy with relief, and if she weren't so spent from crying she might break into sobs right now, but instead she holds her boy's head to her chest, buries her nose in his honey-colored hair, takes in his sweet earthen smell, like a plant used to heal a wound, something restorative, revitalizing.

> **Q:** Assuming that Ashley is 78 years old at the time of her death, and that the probability of her having outlived Wayne is 0.63, how many years is she likely to survive him? Bonus: Using the Ebbinghaus equation, R = exp(-t/S), determine the likelihood that Dylan will retain the memory of the accident, if -t is his age at the time of his mother's death, and S is the relative strength of the memory, which is evidenced by its unbidden resurfacing at her funeral when he is 57, its presence in his mind enough to make him flinch as Father Figgis reads from Ecclesiastes, the man's grainy voice somehow thrusting Dylan back into that moment: his mother's hand on the back of his head, the feel of her sweat-dampened shirt against his cheek, which recollection is accompanied by the fleeting but nonetheless compelling understanding that none of our protections are everlasting, our defenses are only temporary, and that the world, for all that we invest in it, feels nothing for us in return.

7. Is he flying? Floating? Falling? He senses the flurry of activity all around him, doctors and nurses scurrying through his periphery, the banks of machines beeping and hissing, but he's only aware of it in the dimmest reaches of his mind. Someone is tugging on his shirt—no, not tugging. Cutting it off like wrapping paper. Remotely, he's aware of his exposed gut slumped against his belt buckle, which is soon also removed, along with his pants, until he's lying there in his jockeys. Through a cognitive fog that, unbeknownst to him, has been brought about by an intracranial hemorrhage, he observes the team of scrub-clad figures tending to him, only the more he watches the more detached he feels from the bulky body on the gurney: who is that man with the bloodied torso and the crooked, unshaven jaw, the faded pinup girl tattoos which, if given the chance, he might reconsider? Even semiconscious he knows he should be panicking, but instead the thought that comes to mind, unaccountably, is the skydiving instructor calling him an asshole after they had reached the ground. He'd grumbled it as Rick was escorting Sierra back toward the hangar. Rick might have knocked the dude's teeth down his throat were it not for Sierra, who insisted that he just leave it alone, as well as the lingering high from his 120-mile-per-hour freefall, which left him feeling cheerful for the rest of the day, and if only there was some way to hold onto to that feeling all the time, that sensation of plummeting toward the earth, unencumbered, except even joy is too unwieldy to sustain for long, better to unburden oneself of whatever tethers you to this life, although now they are shocking him with a defibrillator, each jolt like an off-note in an otherwise glorious chorus, a hairline crack in a resplendent *hallelujah*, until finally the jolting stops, the chorus quieting, and it's just him, and all of his aimless *wanting* dissipates like mist burning off the earth at sunrise, and here comes the ground, closer, closer, the trees and roads and houses coming into focus, cars inching along winding residential streets, the air blasting in his ears loud as an

engine's roar, and he knows what he's supposed to do, pull the cord, it's so easy, except no, that's not his decision to make anymore, is it?

> Q: Had Rick left Sierra's ten seconds later, had he never lent her his computer, had wind speed been great enough to limit his own velocity, had Ashley given the green light an extra moment or two before inching forward, or had she taken Dylan to the playground before the trip to Kroger, as had been her initial plan until realizing that they were out of fajita seasoning, which they would need for dinner tonight, or had it rained, one of the spur-of-the-moment thundershowers that are common this time of year, or if the Kia that Rick had been tailing for three miles changed lanes an instant sooner, thereby revealing Ashley's RAV in his path, or had there been a hurricane, tornado, wildfire, earthquake, tsunami, had the earth's rotation inexplicably slowed, causing gravity to abate, or if it had hastened, sure, or had the moon vanished and with it its authority over the tides as well the planet's axial stability, what is the likelihood of the accident having been avoided?
>
> A. High
> B. Moderate
> C. Low
> D. Not enough information available to determine

Reunion

1. Age

After weeks of strategizing in Facebook Messenger, they had agreed to meet in a hotel bar in Charleston. *It's a great city*, he'd told her, adding a smile emoji. *You'll love the architecture.*

As if this was supposed to be an educational excursion, she'd thought wryly when he'd proposed it months earlier. She knew he was treading carefully: he didn't want to put in writing their real reason for their meetup—who knew where those messages went once they were typed out?—and for that she was grateful. Still, she had to fight the urge to remind him that she'd already agreed, he didn't need to keep selling her on it.

At the moment, she sat at a cocktail table in the Renaissance Hotel bar, sipping a dirty martini to calm her nerves and watching the bright, cavernous lobby for his arrival. From the ceiling hung helix-shaped droplights, reflected in the smooth tile floor. Through the glass doors, she could see the red-vested valets standing around outside, waiting for vehicles to ferry. She'd always loved hotels, the sense of adventure that came with them. Before the kids, she and Jim used to take weekend trips out of town to lounge around in cushy rooms, having sex and ordering room service. They'd go out to dinner, maybe dancing, but for her the real appeal of the trip was the hotel itself. It was a place to spoil yourself, pretend your life had turned out exactly as you'd planned. And already that afternoon, after a walk through the historic neighborhoods, past the gothic revival houses painted in bright pastels and the festive palmettos lining the sidewalks, she had taken a long soak in the tub and painted her toenails. Now here she was on her second drink and it wasn't even 5 PM. Indulgent, sure, but a little self-care never hurt anyone, had it?

That, anyway, was what she'd told herself the entire four-hour drive from Raleigh, that it was something she'd earned. Besides, it wasn't like she was here to meet some stranger she'd come across online. He was someone she'd loved once, a man who had always understood her, and at forty-four this was all she really wanted.

It had been over twenty years since they'd last seen each other, and both had crafted their own lives, their own families. Then, a year ago, he'd tracked her down online, and they had been chatting regularly ever since, always late at night after their spouses and kids had gone to bed. Reckless though it may have been, it made her feel young again, full of caprice. His photo albums painted a picture of a contented suburbanite father—not exactly the life she would have imagined for the disaffected art major she'd once known, but who was she to make judgments? He was heavier now, not *fat* exactly but *pudgy* for sure, though not in an unattractive way. In fact, she was pleased to see that his metabolism had finally slowed. Back in college he'd been slim bordering on skinny, and his inability to put on weight regardless of what he ate had made him self-conscious. *Oh, poor baby*, she used to tease, not entirely joking, to which he'd flash her that lopsided grin of his, as if this was the reaction he was going for. His hair, dark and wavy, was now threaded with grey, making him seem learned, experienced. She knew plenty of men who dyed their hair, and it always struck her as petty, like how she used to slather her pimples with concealer when she was a teenager, which only made the problem more noticeable. Better to own your age than to fight it, that was her philosophy now. And from what she could tell from his pictures, he owned it well.

By the time she saw him step off the elevator, the woozy calmness of the vodka had begun to settle over her. She glanced at her phone one last time for any messages from Jim or the boys, and then quickly adjusted her bra before he spotted her. He wore a checked shirt and a blazer that was a bit too snug, and he had the inklings of an ash-colored beard. While his size made him seem stately and masculine in his pictures, in person he appeared somewhat oafish, the beard lending his face an unseemly puffiness. Nonetheless, as he waved to her and began lumbering her way, she returned it with a finger flutter that she hoped was the right mixture of friendly and flirty, and it was only then that she realized she was still wearing her ring.

2. Faith

He saw her slip it off and stow it in her pocketbook as he was maneuvering around the other tables, muttering apologies each time he bumped someone with his hip. More and more, his body was beginning to feel like a foreign vessel, something cheaply made and in dire need of new parts. *Time is a cruel joke*, he'd said during one of their online chats, after a couple too many glasses of pinot grigio, which tended to make him melancholy. *It turns us into caricatures of ourselves.*

To which she'd replied, *what the hell r u talking about?*

Now she rose from the table as he approached. She was dressed in a silky blouse and skirt that was probably too short for someone in her mid-forties, though that didn't stop him from momentarily focusing on her shapely legs.

"Oh my god, it's so great to see you!" she squealed, wrapping him in a hug. She smelled good, sugary and clean.

"You too." He stepped back, still holding her hands, his thumb absently sliding over the stripe of bare skin where her ring had been a moment earlier. He'd been careful to leave his on the desk across from the sofa in his room. He didn't want to be caught fiddling with it like he tended to in Dr. Colvin's office, the shrink that Leah had insisted he visit. The doctor had posited that this habit was an indicator of the discomfort he felt over his role as a husband and father—although the man also collected PEZ dispensers of all things, which he kept in a display case in his office, so how much stock did his words really carry? He added, "You look amazing."

"Oh, jeez, well, thanks. I wasn't sure what to wear. They don't make fashion guides for this sort of thing." A nervous giggle, a moment of awkward quiet. "But look at you! You look the exact same."

He thanked her, knowing this wasn't true—he'd packed on at least forty pounds since she'd last seen him—but he appreciated it all the same. As for her, she really did look the same, which was comforting but also a little annoying considering how much she'd complained in their chats about her body being ruined after giving birth to two kids. As far as he could tell she was still as fit as she had been when they were nineteen. The only difference, other than a few laugh lines around her lips, was the hair, which she had also complained about, or rather she'd complained about her husband's response to it, the two-hundred-dollar red highlights, how he'd said it made her head look like a peppermint. And actually, he could sort of see where the man was coming from, though he would never admit this to her.

He ordered a glass of Glenmorangie. He would have preferred

a beer, but he was hoping the scotch would make him come across as suave and interesting, even if it would likely give him killer heartburn later on.

"How sophisticated," she teased when the waitress delivered their drinks.

"I am nothing if not elegant."

"A real caballero."

"What's that?"

"I heard it in a movie somewhere," she said. "Means 'gentleman' or 'knight,' I think. Something like that."

"You have a little too much faith in me. I've never even ridden a horse."

They clinked their glasses together. For a while they played it safe, swapping stories about work. He was a software developer, she a real estate attorney. That neither of them enjoyed their jobs gave them something to bond over—incompetent coworkers, tyrannical bosses, the challenge of balancing a full-time job with a family. From there they moved onto the subject of their kids. She told him about scouting colleges with her son Adam, and about her other son Isaac's recently diagnosed learning disability. He chimed in whenever appropriate, carrying on the innocent pretense of two old friends catching up, though the absence of their spouses from the conversation was impossible to ignore. When talking about her family, he noticed, she was careful to refer to the four of them as a singular unit, *we*, *us*, never mentioning the husband by name, as though doing so might somehow summon the man like a genie. She'd always been the craftier of the two of them, which in a way made her having become a lawyer—a *real estate* lawyer for God's sake—a bit disappointing. It seemed like the kind of career you turned to when you couldn't think of anything else.

When it was his turn, he told her about his daughter Kayla's interest in becoming an influencer.

“What’s that?” she asked.

“I’m honestly not sure. From what I can tell, it just means someone with a YouTube channel.” Kayla was sixteen, a sour-faced C student who, as of late, had taken to calling him by his first name.

She nodded in a resigned way. “I’m so out of that loop, you know? YouTube and TikTok and all that. I don’t really get it.”

“Same here. It all seems really impersonal. I think at this point technology is just pushing us apart.”

“I don’t know if I’d go that far,” she said, shrugging with one shoulder. “I just think that eventually you lose the ability to understand new concepts.”

He grinned. “You think I sound like a bitter old man?”

“I think we’ve both earned the right to be old and bitter,” she said with a wan smile of her own.

He could feel them slipping back into their old dynamic, that playful contention, and it was reassuring, like an old jacket that still fit perfectly after years of use. After all this time, he was pleased to find that the chemistry was still there. And yet, something still felt off. He’d sensed it the entire way from Jacksonville, that he was chasing after something illusory. This city, the hotel, none of it seemed right. Even his room seemed peculiar, like some sort of mockup, the blasé art on the walls telegraphing its falsity, especially the framed print over the desk, directly opposite the bed. It depicted a man in a flannel jacket, as shown from behind, trudging up a snowy hill, a loping bloodhound at his side. Generic hotel art, barely worth noticing. Nonetheless, for twenty minutes he’d stared at the painting, studying the hasty brush strokes, the blobs of color affecting the shapes of leafless trees, unable to pinpoint what bothered him about it.

Likely it wasn’t the painting itself but the guilt that had been festering in his gut ever since he’d agreed to meet her here. Hadn’t he always had a habit of projecting his emotions onto other people or things?

When he and Leah argued, he dealt with his frustration by making repairs around the house, broken appliances and leaky faucets, doors that wouldn't close properly, or by cleaning out the closets, getting rid of old clothes and clutter. He suspected Dr. Colvin would have a lot to say about his fixation with the painting, though the last thing he needed was to offer up more ammo to the man. Not everything was meant to be shared—everyone needed a secret or two.

3. Pressure

She, too, had been to her share of mental health professionals over the years, first after her parents' divorce when she was eleven, her mother having sent her and her two sisters to a child psychologist, but she was always too distracted by the bald little man's unruly nose hairs to absorb anything he said. In college, she'd visited the university counseling center a handful of times when she thought she might be depressed, and then there was the counselor she and Jim had tried a few years ago, a stern woman with unstylish horn-rimmed glasses who had made them sit facing each other and parrot everything the other said.

"I feel like nothing I do is good enough for you," Jim would say, looking coldly into her eyes.

"You're saying that nothing you do is good enough for me," she would repeat.

"I *feel* that way, I'm not saying that's the case."

"Okay, you *feel* that way."

"Now I feel like you're mocking me."

"Now you feel like I'm mocking you."

Despite the antagonism both had initially brought to the sessions, it had ended up working for a while. They became more mindful about raising their voices in the boys' presence, and they even followed the woman's advice to offer each other a compliment at least once a day. But the effort it took to be civil eventually proved too difficult, and it wasn't long after the sessions had stopped that they were back to their old routine of avoidance and silent brooding—which in a lot of ways was preferable, because at least now they didn't feel the pressure to have something glowing on hand to say to the other. No longer did she have to compliment his shirts or listen to him tell her how good she was at, say, loading the dishwasher. They came to a kind of truce, remaining cordial around the boys but spending the rest of their time apart, and she was okay with this.

Which, she reasoned, should have made her absconding to Charleston feel liberating. A chance to *feel* something again, to be touched, desired. She'd already made up her mind that she was going to have sex with him, had fantasized about it for weeks. His hands on her body, his lips. But all that obsessing had come to make it feel obligatory, like an appointment she couldn't break. Or, she *could*, but what would be the point? She'd always been proud of her tenacity, her insistence on following things through to the end—why should this be any different?

They had been in the bar for nearly two hours, according to the clock over the doorway. Having exhausted their list of benign topics, they started trading stories about their college days, people they'd known, youthful indiscretions they'd shared. He reminded her about the time they had fucked in a closet at a house party.

"I forgot all about that!" she lied.

At some point during their reminiscing their hands migrated to the center of the table, and now he stroked the back of her thumb. "So," he said, "did you tell Jim you were coming here?" His voice was low, silky with booze.

"I told him I was going to have a day to myself. Which is the truth."

"What did he say?"

"Nothing really. He's just happy to have me out of the house for a night."

With his free hand, he traced the rim of his glass. "Do you think he suspects anything?"

"I'm not even sure he would care at this point." In fact, it had crossed her mind to tell her husband the truth, mostly just to see if his reaction accorded with what she'd predicted. Except, that seemed a step too far. Regardless of their indifference toward each other, rubbing her infidelity in his face felt cruel. She was a failure as a wife, she could accept this; what she couldn't accept was being a failure as *a person.*

Off to her right, just over his shoulder, an elderly man with thick coke bottle glasses was stealing a bite of food off his wife's plate. They were sitting adjacent to each other, dressed like churchgoers. The woman gave his hand a swat, and they smiled at each other. An act they'd played out countless times. To her surprise, it set off a pang of longing in her.

"Are we bad people?" she heard herself say, a near-murmur, as she watched the moony couple out of the corner of her eye.

"What do you mean?"

"I mean, are we bad for being here? Together?"

"I don't believe in bad people."

She rolled her eyes. "That's not what I asked."

"Are you having second thoughts?" he asked, lacing his thick fingers through hers. "Because it's okay if you are. I don't want there to be any pressure, you know?" He manufactured a smile, but there was no disguising the concern in his voice that she might call the whole thing off, none of the brazen hotel room sex they had intimated. It made her embarrassed for him. For all their bravado, men were just big exposed nerves.

"I'm not," she responded. "I think I'm just anxious."

"About what?"

Good question. What, after all, was there to be anxious about? Jim was three hundred miles away, probably binge-watching *Game of Thrones* in his boxers. She was in an unfamiliar city surrounded by people who didn't know her, didn't give a damn what she did. So what was the problem?

"About whatever *this* is, I guess," she answered. "You have to admit it's kind of crazy."

"Sure, but maybe a little craziness is what we both need."

"You're not nervous? Like, at all?"

He gave her hand a squeeze. "No. I feel like my whole life has been building to this."

She smiled, though she would have just as soon gagged, it was such a saccharine line. But he was *trying*, she had to give him that. Trying to entertain the fantasy they'd concocted, trying to live the life he believed he was owed. Wasn't that why they were here to begin with? Downing the last of her drink in a single gulp, she cast one last look at the elderly couple, who were now engaged in a serious discussion, the man gesticulating with his fork and the woman nodding deeply as if he was confirming some grand truth, and then signaled the waitress for the check, all at once certain that if it didn't happen now, she would lose her resolve.

"I think we better go up to your room," she whispered.

4. Risk

It wasn't true—of course he was nervous, who wouldn't be? His armpits were damp, and he couldn't stop bouncing his knee under the table. Plus, he could feel his face getting hot and blotchy from the scotch. Of course, he'd known he would feel this way, had even discussed it with Dr. Colvin. The doctor, who had a runner's long, lanky build and a bristly beard *a la* Fidel Castro, had listened intently, cocking his head to the side like a dog. "I can see why you'd be apprehensive," the man said. "It's a big chance you're taking."

"Not *that* big." As he'd already explained to the doc, there was a cybersecurity convention in Charleston that weekend, which was why he'd suggested it in the first place. Plausible deniability.

"Big enough for you to tell me about it."

"You can't let Leah know about this, right? Everything stays in this room?"

"I wonder why you're worried about that?" The doc said this in the placating manner of a teacher addressing a struggling student.

"Because she'd kill me if she found out."

"And yet you told me. Quite a risk, yes?"

He let out an exasperated sigh, glancing at the tiered rack of PEZ dispensers on the far wall, which altogether resembled a studio audience. There was Buggs Bunny and the Alien and Santa Claus and the entire Simpsons clan, watching him. "I wanted your opinion. That's your job, isn't it?"

"It's not my job to give you permission." The doctor grinned, but there was no humor in it. "You're looking for approval of your actions, because you know it's a bad idea."

And yet, here he was now, on the elevator with her, the two of them unsteady on their feet, locked in a lusty stare, him caressing her smooth forearm with the backs of his fingers, so what did Dr. Colvin know, really? Maybe it was true that he'd been looking for someone to give him the go-ahead on the Charleston trip, okay fine. But was it possible that it was worth going through with it *because* it was such a bad idea? Who's to say which risks are worth taking? Not everything was to be taken at face value. It was like the painting he'd puzzled over for so long, that faceless old man and his dog: some things just refused to make themselves clear. You had to work to understand them, but even that didn't guarantee that you would.

He considered this now as they stumbled out of the elevator, into the long carpeted hallway. He was dizzy, though it wasn't all from the liquor. Stopping in front of his door, he leaned in and pressed his mouth to hers. It had been years since he'd kissed with any intensity, and it felt a little inelegant, as though his lips had been anesthetized. Nevertheless, she gripped his back, ran her hand up his nape, buried her cold fingers in his hair.

Are we bad people?

He could recall her saying something similar on their first date. He'd taken her to a chain restaurant near the university, one of these places with ancient sports paraphernalia all over the walls; it was all he could afford. The meal had gone surprisingly well, both of them opening up to the other in ways they hadn't anticipated. She'd told him about her parents' separation, her mother making her way through a series of lowlife boyfriends for years afterward, musicians and tattoo artists and the like, the polar opposite of her staid father. His parents had also divorced, he told her, though they'd remained amicable. He and his sister would bounce weekly between their father's McMansion in the suburbs and their mother's quaint farmhouse on the edge of the county.

"You're lucky," she'd said, her chin in her hand. "It could be so much worse."

He'd bobbed his head in agreement, not sure if she was referring to his family arrangements or something larger, harder to define.

When they'd gotten in his car to leave, they discovered that the battery had died. The car was a junky hand-me-down Honda from his sister, and the corroded battery was likely as old as the vehicle itself. As embarrassed as he'd been, though, he was delighted to have more time alone with her. As they'd waited for someone leaving the restaurant to give him a jump, she'd kissed him, a hasty maneuver that caught him off-guard. Her mouth tasted thrillingly of the mint she'd plucked from a bowl on the hostess stand. Then, after a couple minutes, she pulled back as though he'd done something to offend her. "What is it?" he said, breathless.

"I just can't believe I'm doing this."

"Why?"

She squinted at him like the question didn't make sense. In the dimness of the car, the parking lot lights emphasized the contours of her face, the tender curve of her cheek, the severe jut of her chin. "It's only a first date." Then, after a beat, "God, am I a terrible person?"

At the time, he'd found it charming, her need to be reassured of her virtue, her tone equal parts concerned and demure. But now, more than two decades later, as he fumbled in his pocket for the room key, the question—*Are we bad people?*—struck him as manipulative, unfair. It felt like a test, only there was no correct answer.

5. Familiarity

Into the suite they staggered, through the small foyer, which gave way to the living room area and, beyond that, the massive bed, festooned with creamy white pillows, his beard scratching her face and neck like a scouring pad. The place had that stale hotel smell, disinfectant and carpet deodorizer, years of bodies moving in and out. They fell onto the bed, his teeth clacking against hers, and she let out a grunt of discomfort.

"You okay?" he said.

"Yeah. Just rusty, you know?"

He nodded, though she doubted he had any idea what she meant. Intimacy wasn't the same for men; they weren't burdened by the same expectations. Women just weren't hardwired for lust. Or no, that wasn't it—*she* wasn't. When was the last time she had actually enjoyed sex? She couldn't say, nor could she say whether this suggested more about Jim, the only person she'd been with for twenty years, or her. In any event, she was suddenly, *glaringly* aware that she was alone in a hotel room with a man she hadn't seen in over two decades, aware of his sizeable body atop hers, of the piney tang of his cologne, the hard pressure of his erection on her hip.

He stroked her arm. It made her stiffen, as if it was a stranger touching her, though he didn't seem to notice. "It really is good to see you."

"You too," she replied, putting a hand on his furry cheek.

"It's so weird to think of you as a lawyer now, you know?"

She angled her head back. "Why?"

"No, I didn't mean—I just meant because it's weird how things turn out, you know? Like, how we are totally different people now. That's all I'm saying."

"I suppose." Her hand fell from his face.

"Did I upset you?"

"No, it's fine."

"I've upset you."

"It's okay."

She kissed him again, reassuringly, but her enthusiasm was waning. It wasn't just the crack about her being a lawyer that bothered her—and, justly or not, it *did* bother her—but the dawning understanding that he would never live up to the version of him she'd crafted in her mind. That version was smooth and confident and always had something clever to say; when he kissed her, it was skillfully romantic, like something out of a movie—his tongue didn't worm around inside her mouth, sour with alcohol. And while she knew that this wasn't his fault, something in her was determined to be indignant. To hold him accountable.

Wriggling out from under him, she came to her feet. "Be right back," she chirped, scurrying to the bathroom. She could feel his eyes on her as she shut the door behind her.

Bracing her hands on the faux-marble basin, she looked herself over in the mirror, adjusted the hem of her skirt, fussed with her hair. Anything to help kickstart the mood, but the more she primped, the older and more alone she felt. She thought about the elderly couple in the bar, that rapport that only comes from decades of devotion. She wanted to be at home. She missed her boys. She even found herself pining for Jim a little. Despite all evidence to the contrary, familiarity did have its charms.

It wasn't until she decided to reapply her lipstick that she realized she'd left her pocketbook down in the bar. In their drunken rush to get upstairs, it hadn't even occurred to her to grab it. Ordinarily, this might have sent a wave of distress crashing over her—her credit cards were in it, after all, not to mention her phone and, yes, her ring—but to her dismay the first thing she felt was relief: it would give her a reason to leave the room.

6. Footprints

Of course, she'd never been the subtle type, and he could sense her ambivalence as soon as she reentered the room. Even as she explained about the pocketbook, he could tell she was pleased for a reprieve. Which only amplified his own insecurities. Had he come on too strong? Was she repulsed by his size, as he'd feared she might be? In the bar she'd been so confident, almost impertinent in her flirtations. But something had shifted, that much was clear: she was holding back, and he wasn't sure he had the strength to draw it out of her, whatever it was. Or if she even wanted him to.

Again, there was that feeling of incompleteness that he'd experienced upon his arrival, like he'd made a misstep that would only reveal itself later, when it was too late.

"I can grab it and come back," she said, smoothing down her blouse and skirt.

"Okay." He was propped up on his elbows, his erection withering.

"I'm sorry. I'll only be a few minutes."

"No problem."

He watched her struggle to slip on her plum-colored pumps. She was trying not to look at him. At last she flashed him a quick, business-like smile and turned toward the door, only to pause mid-step. "That's weird," she said.

"What is?"

She motioned toward the painting. "There aren't any footprints."

Now he sat up straight on the bed. "What do you mean?"

"In the picture. Look, there aren't any."

Leaning forward, he examined the painting. She was right—there were no footprints in the snow behind the man. No indication of his progress up the hill.

"I'll be damned," he said, more to himself.

"Kind of a strange thing to leave out, don't you think?"

The offhanded way she said it made it sound as minor as an errant brush stroke; chances were she'd forget about it as soon as she left the room. But to him it was anything but minor. It was like the solution to a problem he'd been dwelling on for ages had just presented itself to him, and all at once he flashed back to their breakup so many years prior. They had been together for two years, though there had been a number of rough patches during which the relationship had been halted, or at least it had felt this way to him. In any event, it had all culminated in the two of them standing in the parking lot of her apartment complex one evening in early spring, mosquitoes and no-see-ums zipping around their heads, while she tearfully told him that she just couldn't do it anymore, it was over. "I think we like the idea of each other better than we like each other," she'd said, gazing off toward the road as if waiting for someone to swoop in and save her.

When he'd told this story to Dr. Colvin last week, the doctor had nodded and asked, "So, what makes you think anything has changed after all this time?"

"We're different people now."

"How so?"

He'd opened his mouth to answer, but he couldn't come up with a response, at least not one that felt truthful. Strange. Surely, there had to be differences between who he was then and who he was now—there *had* to be, right? Only, for the life of him he couldn't think of what they were.

Now, gazing at the painting, that patch of white that should have been marred by footprints, by the insinuation of progress, he said to her, "I can't believe no one ever caught that."

But when he glanced in her direction, he saw that she was gone. Which, he realized, was probably for the best. She wasn't coming back, he knew this, and yet amazingly it didn't faze him. In fact, he was actually okay with that—the realization of which startled him, just like she had when she'd suggested they go upstairs. Some things you can see coming a mile away and still find yourself stunned once they arrive. Which was why he now turned his attention back to the painting, watching it raptly like a museum patron, wondering what else he'd overlooked.

7. Possibility

By the time she made it back to the bar, her buzz was already burning off, leaving her feeling tired and morose. Yet, as bad as she felt about running out on him, she was glad to be in the presence of other people again, even if it was just diners chattering over their meals. She found the pocketbook, a honey-colored leather clutch, in the chair where she had left it; the waitress must have missed it when she bussed the table. Quickly, she rifled through it to make sure that everything was accounted for and then, with a feeling like she was locking a door she would never reopen, slipped her ring back on. And it was then that she noticed the elderly couple was gone. The remnants of a slice of chocolate-drizzled cheesecake sat on a small dish in the center of their table, between a pair of wine glasses, a splash of red left at the bottom of each.

If their table hadn't been bussed yet, that must mean she had only just missed them. Hailing a waitress, she asked when they had left. "Just a couple minutes ago, I think," the woman responded.

"Did they leave the hotel or go upstairs?"

"Went home, probably." The woman was heavyset, her plump face caked in makeup that had begun to crack like dried clay. "They come in all the time."

After the waitress had sauntered away, she hustled out into the lobby. Not that she had any idea of what she might even say to the couple—maybe nothing, she just needed to see them again, that dreamy cast in their eyes. In all likelihood, they were already headed back to their cozy bungalow to climb into bed together, maybe doze off in front of the TV, warm beneath a heavy comforter. That, anyway, was the image she'd contrived of them.

She thought about him waiting for her upstairs. She, too, could recall their first date, the exhilaration of kissing a handsome boy with whom she had so much in common, the gleeful suggestion of possibility. She'd been trying to run down that moment ever since, hadn't she? Yes, she supposed she had, just like him, but then again, didn't everybody need something to chase?

This was why she now burst through the revolving door out onto the sidewalk, into the blush of early evening, where she was greeted by the bustle of bodies. The air, thick and warm, was fragrant with the greasy aroma of food from the nearby restaurants, the moon peeking just over the skyline. She elbowed her way around guests toting roller bags and backpacks, past weary-looking parents wrangling children, businessmen in starchy shirts blathering into phones. Standing on her tiptoes, she peered over the crush of people. There they were, at the corner, the man hailing a cab, his features made sharp by the coppery glow of a street lamp. The vehicle pulled up to the curb and he opened the car door for his wife, who folded her small figure into the back, the man now gingerly stepping off the sidewalk to join her, and if only the crowd weren't so dense, or if she'd left the room a moment sooner. If only she could reach them before they were gone.

Landfall

By the time Nicole arrives at the clinic, the parking lot is already full of folks waiting to drop off their pets before hightailing it out of town, out of the path of the hurricane. All morning she's been battling that crampy twinge in her hand—*dystonia*, Dr. Epstein, her neurologist, calls this, involuntary muscle contractions—and she hoped that she would be able to spend most of today hiding in her office. A foolish hope, it turns out, considering that all of the pet-friendly hotels within a hundred-mile radius have already sold out. Unlocking the front doors, she marshals a smile as the sleepy-eyed clients slump into the lobby with their cat carriers and their leashed dogs.

Inside, she leaves the receptionist to check everyone in while she goes around the building flicking on lights. In the fusty-smelling kennel at the back of the building, she feeds and waters the dozen or so animals already boarding and begins taking the dogs outside one by one. Technically, this is a job for the assistants, but the traffic is likely to make them late, and anyway as owner Nicole takes a sheepish sort of pleasure in micromanaging. A canopy of gunmetal clouds hangs low in the sky, the wind already churning ominously. By tomorrow afternoon, the rains will be here, thick and driving. Initial projections had the hurricane cutting west, into the Gulf of Mexico. Perhaps Nicole shouldn't have been surprised when the projections abruptly shifted, the storm now expected to hook northeast, right through the Carolinas. That's her life in a nutshell, isn't it? A sudden change in trajectory, something to brace for. *You're just feeling sorry for yourself,* her mother might scold, caustic old bird that she was, and of course she would be right. But her mother is long gone, and so who cares if Nicole is feeling a little morose this morning? It's her clinic, she can feel whatever the hell she wants.

She waits until all the other dogs have been walked before taking out the rottweiler that Animal Control dropped off yesterday. It was found near the airport, a scrawny female with patchy fur and a missing chunk of ear. Upon being hustled into the van, the animal bit one of the officers on the hand. "Fucker cost me three stitches," the fellow said when he dropped the dog off, holding up his bandaged hand for Nicole to see.

"Three's not so bad," she replied, gently releasing the rottweiler from the restraining pole. When the animal didn't attack her, just regarded Nicole with a toddler's look of expectant curiosity, she was both relieved and a little let down: you expect wild things to act like wild things. "I've definitely seen worse."

The officer, his khaki shirt straining against the bulge of his belly, rubbed his mangled hand, perturbed by the lack of sympathy. "Know what's better than three? None."

Unfortunately, the attack means that the dog has to be put down, her head sent to the state CDC office for rabies testing. It's a cruel catch-22, having to kill a creature to determine if it's sick, and if the dog's pleasant demeanor is any indication—tongue lolling friskily, stumpy tail wagging as Nicole slips on the leash—she isn't. Nevertheless, by state law Nicole has until the end of the day to euthanize the animal and remove the head, a task she isn't looking forward to, which is why she's been putting it off until the last minute.

She leads the dog out the back door, around the side of the building, the animal pausing to piss on a clump of weeds, and toward the thicket of trees on the far side of the parking lot. The dog's ribs are visible through her black fur, but she moves with a merry trot, as though she and Nicole are old friends. Hard to believe this creature could harm anything, let alone a human being, but backed into a corner who knows what any living thing is capable of. As the animal investigates the flowerbeds at the front of the building, Nicole watches the dogwoods rustle in the winds. It's September, a mild crispness in the air that sets off a pang of longing in her, as if she's preparing herself for a great loss. Which, in a way, she is. Her retirement from the clinic, from veterinary medicine altogether, is inevitable, despite the fact that she is only forty—the only question is *when*. That she hasn't stepped away from the practice already could be construed as reckless, but how do you just walk away from something you've worked so diligently to build up? When Nicole took over the clinic from Dr. Farmer six years ago after he quite publicly burnt out ("I'm just ready to start drowning pugs," she once overheard him grumble to a client), it was a modestly successful practice that, due to the doctor's cantankerous aversion to advertising, was little known outside of the league of geriatrics to whom he'd spent most of his career catering. Now it's one of the most high-profile animal clinics in the region, boasting contracts with the sheriff's department and the police and fire departments. (Nicole personally capped all seven of the county's new drug-sniffing German Shepherds' teeth with titanium sheaths, the fact of which received a half-page write-up in the Wilmington *Star-News*.) So, what is she supposed to do, just turn her back on the whole thing as if it's a project she's grown bored with?

Jessica, one of the techs, exits the lobby and strolls across the parking lot to let her know her first appointment is waiting in Room 1. "Jeez, it's like the end of days out here," she remarks, gazing warily up at the darkening sky. Eddies of leaves whirl past them as if running for their lives.

"'But concerning that day and hour no one knows, not even the angels of heaven, nor the Son, but the Father only'," Nicole recites. When Jessica narrows her eyes at her quizzically, she says, "Matthew 24:36."

"I know the verse. I just never took you for a bible scholar. No offense."

Nicole shrugs. "Scholar, no. But I did go to Catholic school."

"That'll do it, I guess."

"You gotta love that Old Testament attitude," Nicole says. "So doom and gloom."

"Matthew is in the New Testament."

"Yeah, but it doesn't belong there."

Jessica futzes with her long black ponytail. She wears kitten-patterned scrubs and a silver cross around her neck. Despite her familiarity with the bible, Nicole has never been religious, has never understood the appeal of prayer. Everything has an explanation, that's just science; there is no need to bring God into the equation. And yet, there is a contentedness to the believers she knows, the church-goers and the bible thumpers, that she can't help envying. Like Jessica, they always seem so self-assured, so breezy, as though they long ago resigned themselves to whatever the future has in store for them. She wonders how their outlooks might change if they knew for certain what it was.

"Also," Jessica goes on, "Andy called, says he and Marcy and the kids are evacuating, can't come in this morning."

"Something tells me we'll survive." Nicole expected this, her employees calling out, skittish about the storm. Any other day this would annoy her, but today she doesn't mind, especially in the case of Andy, a lumbering lout who spends most of his shifts out back chain-smoking and who travels in a pungent cloud of men's body spray that fails to cover up his BO. Losing him for the day will probably make things easier for everyone.

"Actually," Jessica continues, "I was going to see if it was okay if I took off a little early today? I want to get out of town before the traffic gets bad. Do you mind?"

"I guess not."

"I mean, I can stay if you want."

"It's fine, Jessica. The governor's supposed to issue an evacuation order anyway. You should go."

"Okay, thank you, Nicole." She puts a hand on Nicole's shoulder. The rottweiler sniffs idly at her crotch. "I'll be praying for you."

"Let me know how that works out," Nicole mumbles, immediately regretting it—the girl is just trying to be kind—but Jessica, already turning to go back inside, doesn't hear.

•

Living in Wilmington, you get used to hurricanes, or at least you are supposed to. You stock up on food and batteries and hope that your impact windows hold. But this one, Hurricane Florence, feels different. It's expected to make landfall as a category 4. Major news networks are already calling it the "storm of the century," a phrase that strikes Nicole as painfully outmoded. She can't help feeling a thorn of resentment over the fact that her clients get to evacuate while she is stuck tending to their pets. But someone has to keep the animals fed, and she isn't going to stop her stable of vet techs, a few of whom—like Andy—have small children at home, from fleeing town with everyone else. She isn't that kind of boss.

Actually, she's still figuring out what kind of boss she is. Before taking over the clinic, she was a partner for ten years, joining straight out of vet school. Sixteen years of experience, more than enough for her to feel like she knows what she is doing, and yet even now she can't shake the sense that she is faking it, an imposter who weaseled her way into her position. A lot of this has to do with the fact that she still looks like she is at least ten years younger, with her compact frame and perky cheekbones and the scattering of freckles across her nose. Most of her friends would kill to be mistaken for a twenty-something, as happens to Nicole regularly. But few of them have real careers; most are stay-at-home moms who peddle Scentsy to keep from dying of boredom. They don't have to worry about being taken seriously, not like she does. *Are you sure you're old enough to be a doctor?* her clients will sometimes say, not necessarily joking. Nicole long ago stopped reassuring them that she knows what she's doing. All she can do now is give a bland smile as if to suggest that she too is baffled that anyone would hand over a veterinary degree to a pixie like her.

Then there is *this*—this, what? Illness? Curse? Despite its name, Huntington's seems too complex, too mystifying to be called a *disease*. Whatever you want to call it, it only compounds the feeling of fraudulence that has characterized her tenure at the clinic, so that it is often hard to determine where her legitimate feelings end and the sickness begins. It makes her wonder if all those years of trying to prove herself were for nothing.

The problems began six months ago. At first, she thought it was just depression. She battled it in college, and so she was no stranger to the weary malaise that settled over her like a cloudy film around her brain. Except, there was more to it this time—bouts of crippling anxiety, as though certain death was imminent; flashes of unreasonable rage, often in regard to something innocuous (a dirty bathtub, an offhanded remark from one of her two sons) and which left her feeling guilty and in need of a drink; moments of embarrassing forgetfulness. (More than once she ended up sitting through green lights, much to the fury of the drivers behind her, because the notion of *going*, bizarrely, just didn't occur to her.)

Looking back, it's surprisingly easy to write these mishaps off as byproducts of the divorce, which took place last spring, instead of the onset of a debilitating sickness. Her brain rebooting itself in the wake of a major life change, that's all it must be. The truth is that she's trying her damndest not to acknowledge the stony realization yawning in the faintest reaches of her mind, that what is happening to her is part of something larger, the same thing that took her mother nearly thirty years before.

In her younger years her mother was spry, crotchety, and sharp-tongued, a nightmare for telemarketers and pushy salesmen. By the end of her life, however, she had degenerated into a shuddering, babbling wreck of a woman wholly dependent upon the staff at the hospice clinic. She couldn't move on her own, save for the constant jerking of her head and limbs, or go to the bathroom or even form words, though the nurses reassured Nicole's family that despite the mental deterioration caused by the disease she was cognizant, still able to understand most of what they were saying to her. To Nicole, however, this made it seem all the more horrific: her mother was a prisoner in her own malfunctioning body, a passenger trapped on a sinking vessel.

It makes sense, then, that for years Nicole deluded herself about the likelihood of facing the same fate—confronting the truth seemed too immense, like solving a riddle whose only reward was death. Until, that is, the incident with the Great Dane puppy. She was pulling out the intestines of the six-month-old dog one morning during a routine spay, trying to get a better look at the uterus, when her hand twitched. A single flicking motion, as though she were dismissing someone, momentary, but enough to make her drop the scalpel, slicing the root of the mesenteric artery. For nearly forty-five minutes she struggled to get the bleeding under control while Jessica, who was assisting, looked on, mortified. That the dog didn't die was a miracle—or so Jessica later proclaimed—and in fact Nicole didn't even tell the owners about the accident. But for days after, it was all she could think about.

Weeks later, at the doctor's office, listening to Dr. Epstein drone on about mutated chromosomes and dominant genes, all Nicole could do was inwardly berate herself for never getting tested for the gene, in spite of her sister Laurie's persistence. "Don't you want to know, just in case?" she'd said. "So you can plan?" No, as a matter of fact, Nicole hadn't wanted to know. Why would she want to spend her adulthood panicking over encroaching convalescence? The coin was already flipped the moment she was born—as a woman of science, she told herself it was only logical to let it fall on its own, without any intervention. What a stupid, immature belief, she can see this now. She's had her entire life to prepare for the illness, which blessedly passed over Laurie, but what did she do? Bank on the wrong odds, that's what, allowing herself to be blindsided. Nothing logical about that at all.

Terminal illness, it turns out, can teach you a lot of things, most of which no healthy person could ever understand. Things you are better off not knowing. And if Nicole has learned anything from the illness so far, it's the insufficiency of language. Knowing what her future holds seems to defy words—*I'm going to die* doesn't even come close. Very few people get to know what's in store for them, but the ones who do wish like hell that they didn't. And so, she's kept it to herself so far, not even telling Garrett or the boys, because no matter how she formulates the explanation in her head, it never feels like enough.

•

At noon during her lunch break, as Nicole is puttering around the treatment room working up the courage to euthanize the rottweiler, Garrett saunters in with the pink cat carrier under one arm, Jinx mewling angrily inside. The treatment room is technically off limits to clients, and while Nicole has never given the receptionists instructions to bar him from that part of the building, she just assumed it was implied. No clients and no ex-husbands.

"Who's this?" he says, motioning toward the dog in her cage. Nicole had to stash her in here because all the runs in the kennel are full.

"A stray. Bound for doggie heaven."

"That's too bad." He holds out his palm. "Hey there, pooch."

The dog gives his hand a tentative sniff through the wires of the cage and then looks up at Nicole as if for reassurance. *I don't know about this guy*, she seems to say.

"Going somewhere?" Nicole asks, indicating the carrier.

"Taking Neil and Sean to my dad's." Garrett's father lives in a roomy colonial outside of Atlanta.

"We didn't talk about that."

"It's my week with them. I didn't have to clear it with you. Besides, don't you want them as far away from here as possible?"

"You could have at least given me a heads up."

"I'm giving you one now."

Nicole sighs. It's all she can do in the face of his presumptuousness, although he is right, she doesn't want the boys in town for the storm. Taking the carrier from Garrett, she dumps the cat into one of the empty treatment cages. Jinx takes a swipe at her and cowers behind the litter box, issuing that low feline rumble that to Nicole always sounds like distant thunder.

A lot of things have changed since the divorce last year, which, to Garrett's credit, was amicable—Nicole moved out, into a condo near the beach; she only sees her sons every other week (perhaps she should be more distraught over this, but after spending a week as a single parent with a twelve-year-old and a thirteen-year-old, she welcomes the next seven days to recuperate); a good number of her friends dropped off the face of the earth, although most of them are the wives of Garrett's work associates, so no big loss there; and Nicole, no longer required to prepare meals for her family, packed on ten pounds from her diet of fast food and microwavable meals. But one thing that hasn't changed is that Garrett continues to bring Jinx to the clinic. Starting over with another doctor, he's explained, would be a pain in the ass. This is one of the many things that has always annoyed Nicole about her ex-husband, his ability to spin his own laziness into an act of prudence, as if he's doing them all a favor by not seeking out a new vet. Not to mention his creepy devotion to the cat, a Maine Coon mix who, from the moment they adopted it, has despised Nicole, always hiding around corners and attacking her ankles. Even now, more than a year after moving out, she still bears scars from the ambushes. That the cat favors Garrett certainly isn't his fault, but she can't deny that it factored into her rationalizing the split.

"That cat's a psycho," she says.

"He just gets scared in new places."

"This isn't a new place, Garrett. Seriously, there's like fifty clinics in this city. You can't go to one of those?"

"He's your cat, too." There is a pouty note in his voice that makes Nicole's bowels clench. Goddamn Garrett, always going for the heart-strings.

"Not anymore. That's not how this works."

He leans against the counter and sighs. A statistics professor at UNC Wilmington, he carries an air of scholarly poise that is both charming and irksome. "I really wish you'd reconsider evacuating," he says. "This thing is supposed to be devastating."

"They say that every year."

"Yeah, but this year they mean it."

"They say that, too."

"You could come with us. Dad's place has plenty of room. I know the boys would love it."

"I appreciate your concern, Garrett, but I can't. We're full up with boarders. And a hundred bucks says the storm is downgraded before it hits."

He shrugs but doesn't push the issue, though she can see that he wants to, some mild rejoinder about her refusal to accept help, perhaps. Their usual song and dance. Nicole studies him, his thin, angular face and whiskey-colored hair parted down the center. She used to joke, to his annoyance, that he looked like a choirboy. She recalls how, long before the divorce, when Neil and Sean were young, she and Garrett would stock the space under the stairs full of boardgames and snacks and drinks, and the four of them would ride out the hurricanes in cozy comfort playing Battleship and Monopoly. When it was over, they would walk the neighborhood, inspecting the damage, the felled trees and scattered limbs, the pieces of siding ripped from houses like old bandages. There was always something reassuring about the scene, the way it reminded them that they were still here, still standing. The storm had passed, and here they were, survivors.

It's one of those moments of somber introspection when they both seem to be sizing each other up, probing for ways in, and she is reminded of what drew them together in the first place and, at the same time, why it didn't last. What might have happened if she had been diagnosed before the divorce? Would they have found a way around their differences? Would Garrett have taken care of her over the course of her illness, or would he have come to resent her for the constant attention she required, her slow degradation right in front of their sons' faces? Either way, Nicole suspects she's better off not knowing. In the back of her head, she can hear her mother's voice again, the same refrain she hears these days whenever she is around Garrett or the boys: *Just tell him. Get it over with.*

She is right, of course, but no, Nicole can't do that to them. It's her burden, not theirs. For the time being, anyway.

If not now, when?

Soon. It needs to be done, of course she understands this, yes. But how do you drop something like that in someone's lap, the father of your children no less? *Oh, by the way, I'm dying.* While she knows it is unfair to keep Garrett out of the loop, bringing him in feels equally ruthless. As for Neil and Sean, she's already lost plenty of sleep over that impending conversation. After all, she was witness to her mother's own slow demise—if anybody knows what that sort of thing does to a kid, it's her.

"You okay?" he says.

"Yeah," replies Nicole. "Why?"

"You had a funny look on your face."

She busies herself with a stack of files on the counter, averting her eyes. "Just zoned out for a minute."

"You should get some rest. You work too much."

It's one of the ongoing points of contention between them, Nicole's obsession with her work, and while she knows that Garrett isn't baiting her, she is still bothered by his having ruined the moment. All he had to do was not talk for a little bit, is that so hard? Why are people so intimidated by silence? Rolling her eyes and exhaling loudly, she worms her fingers through the wires of the rottweiler's cage and scratches the furry folds beneath the animal's jaw.

"Where have I heard that before?" she says.

•

It wasn't just the sight of her mother's contorted form in the wheelchair that made Nicole hate the weekly visits to the hospice clinic when she was young, or the groaning burble of her struggling to speak, or even the arsenal of crushed up medications that the nurses had to force down her throat several times a day because she was incapable of swallowing. It was the antiseptic stink of the room, the lifeless fluorescents humming in the hallway where all day long hunched figures in dingy robes shuffled back and forth like spirits. It was the way everything felt only half there, as if it were in the process of vanishing. This wasn't death, this was something much worse.

"Don't ever let me end up in a place like that," she once proclaimed on the drive home from the clinic. How old had she been? Ten maybe, eleven. She wasn't sure who she was speaking to, her father behind the wheel or Laurie in the passenger's seat. The subject of hers and Laurie's genetic dispositions had been broached once or twice—Nicole understood that her chances of her developing the disease all depended on her genes, though she didn't really know what that entailed—but their father, left alone to raise his two daughters while his wife of twenty years languished in the foul-smelling clinic, hadn't yet had the stomach to explore the matter in any depth, and neither girl had been brave enough to ask.

"We'll cross that bridge," he mumbled.

"I don't want to die in some gross hospital room. I don't want to have to wear a diaper."

"You'll die way before we have to stick you in there," Laurie teased, three years older than Nicole. "Cancer of the butt, that's what gets you."

"Whatever. You're going to get cancer of the face."

"No such thing."

"There's no such thing as cancer of the butt, either."

"Anal cancer. That's a real thing."

"Would you two stop being so morbid?" her father said, a faint tremor in his voice. "Please?"

"I hate that place," Nicole groused. "Seriously, if I ever end up like mom, just kill me."

Jerking the wheel to the right, her father swerved into the parking lot of a pizza restaurant, Nicole and Laurie rocking in their seats. He lurched to a stop and then, twisting around, slapped Nicole across the face. He was a bear of a man, a general contractor who built furniture in his spare time, and his hand felt mammoth, the skin of his palm like aged wood. The slap, which resounded like a gunshot, was forceful enough to knock Nicole sideways, her head bonking against the window.

For a couple minutes nobody spoke. The interior of the car felt tiny, stifling. Behind them, traffic whizzed past. Nicole clutched her stinging cheek, her eyes watering, while Laurie gaped at her as if trying to understand what she had just seen. It was the first time their father had ever laid hands on either of them—to compensate for his considerable size, he was ordinarily soft-spoken and gentle, reluctant to even raise his voice—and from the backseat Nicole could see his face as the realization of what he'd done sunk in, his features stiffening and his cheeks deepening in color. She could tell that he wanted to apologize, to undo the moment, but instead he turned back around to the front and, swiping at his misty eyes, gripped the steering wheel like an anxious first-time driver.

"No one's killing anyone," he grumbled.

•

By late afternoon Nicole is down to just a couple of techs, the rest of her staff having either called off or left early. She spends the remainder of the day taking blood samples and clipping claws and administering heartworms meds and expressing anal glands, rattling off the usual instructions to clients: *Apply twice daily. Wrap it in a piece of bologna before feeding it to her. Try not to let him lick it.* There is a certain rhythm to it all that she has always found comforting, especially during hers and Garrett's last years together, when they could hardly stand to be in the same house as each other and all she had to keep her sane, in addition to her children, was her job. Why humans are considered the pinnacle of evolution, she will never understand: animals make sense in ways that people don't. They don't lie or bicker with you over a diagnosis or make sloppy attempts at flirting during appointments, as happens to Nicole at least a couple times a month, usually by older men with the pall of desperation that tends to cling to the almost-elderly. Sure, animals can be difficult, and over the years she has been mauled by countless frightened pets. But at least that fear is predictable, and more and more a little predictability is all she really wants.

At four o'clock, shortly after the governor's evacuation order for all the counties along the coast, she and the techs nail up sheets of plywood over the floor-to-ceiling lobby windows, making the place look condemned. Holding the hammer proves tricky—she has to grip it with only her pointer and middle fingers, her achy pinky and ring fingers curled inward, useless—but they manage to get the job done within a half hour. When they are finished, Nicole sends them all home. One or two of them extend half-hearted but well-intentioned invitations for her to skip town with their families, all of which she graciously declines. Her condo is far enough away from the beach that flooding shouldn't be an issue, and she has stockpiled enough cases of bottled water and food to last her several weeks. "I'll be just fine," she assures them, and she can see the relief on their faces at her declining their offer.

When it's just her and the animals left in the building, she trudges reluctantly toward the treatment room to finish off the rottweiler. If there is one part of the job she can do without, it's the euthanizations. Somehow, having that kind of control over another living thing has always felt...indecent. How many animals has she put down over the years? Hundreds? Thousands? Enough that this one shouldn't feel any different. But it does. It feels cold-blooded, like it's her own dog she's destroying.

Nicole leads the dog from her cage and leashes her up to the eye-bolt in the wall. She fills a syringe with pentobarbital and a dash of muscle relaxant and then kneels to administer the candy-pink concoction, pulling back on the skin of the dog's leg with her thumb to expose the vein. To her surprise, the rottweiler doesn't protest, just lets her manhandle her as though she has already accepted her fate. Silvery strings of drool drip from her whiskered jowls to the tiled floor. Some animals you can look at and see the contented house pets they might have been in another life, the same way you can tell with certain people that this isn't the path their life was supposed to take. Maybe the rottweiler could have been a farm dog, wrangling sheep alongside some weathered farmer, sitting on the porch in the evenings with a rope toy, secure in the knowledge that she is accepted and loved. Do animals have an inkling of how differently their lives could have turned out? Would they be any better off for it?

This is what Nicole is thinking as she brings the needle to the animal's arm, only to find that her hand is too stiff and sore for her to operate the plunger. She tries shifting positions, readjusting her legs beneath her, but she still can't get her hand to cooperate. Maybe she could switch hands, only she doesn't trust herself to locate a vein with her left. She tries again, but her fingers won't cooperate. As she's struggling to tighten her grasp, the syringe slips from her sweaty grip and clatters onto the floor, rolling toward Jinx's cage. As the rottweiler takes a step forward to sniff it, the cat's paw shoots out with dizzying speed and catches the dog on her nose.

Yelping, she flails backwards, knocking against the cabinets as she paws at her own snout. "Goddammit, Jinx!" Nicole snaps, smacking the cage door, prompting a hiss from the cat. She hunkers down in front of the whimpering dog and strokes her head to calm her. "It's okay," she murmurs, "you're okay." Trembling, the animal allows her to examine the wound. Three scratches, beaded with blood, right down the front of her black muzzle. Grabbing a handful of paper towels, Nicole blots at them.

What's the point? You were about to kill her anyway.

Yes, but sending the animal off with a bleeding wound feels cruel. Doesn't every creature deserve some dignity in death?

Did I?

Of course, but deserving something and actually getting it are two very different things.

As she strokes the dog's fuzzy snout, her thoughts drift back to the day of her mother's funeral, the reception at the house after the burial. Throngs of black-clad mourners mulled around nibbling deviled eggs and chicken salad and sipping from Styrofoam cups of coffee, chattering in whispery voices. While her father smoked on the back porch, Nicole drifted through the room in a daze, enduring the doleful condolences of neighbors and distant family members. *She's in a better place now.* Oh, how she would like to have throttled those people, just wring all the useless platitudes out of them like the last spurts of water out of an old rag. *A better place than with her husband and daughters?* she wanted to say to them. *Is that what you mean?*

When she'd had more than she could handle, she considered going upstairs to Laurie's room, where her sister was hiding out, no doubt getting high, but instead Nicole found herself drifting toward the bathroom. Inside, she looked at herself in the mirror, her prim black dress and clumpy makeup. Shakily, she brought her hand to her cheek, the same cheek that her father had smacked, and she recalled the hot sting of his palm, the way it had whipped her head around like a weathervane, and how for an instant all her thoughts had scattered.

Then she slapped herself. It was light, as though she were smacking at a mosquito, a little too light maybe. When she did it again, she did it harder, her head reverberating with the steely energy of a tuning fork. She did it once more, even harder this time, though she found that she didn't mind the pain—she actually sort of liked it, the way it focused the rabble in her brain into a single point and how, with each successive hit, that point grew finer, more concentrated, her awareness of the world around her shrinking as though she were blacking out, until she was heaving breathlessly over the sink, her cheek the deep coral shade of raw meat, her hand throbbing. Mascara ran down her face in rivulets. Her hair was mussed, her lipstick smeared. She looked like a survivor of some great catastrophe, someone who, despite the odds, had managed to thwart disaster.

Why this memory now surfaces, Nicole has no idea; maybe because it was the first time she understood that pain is the only real certainty in the world. That, fair or not, everybody pays a price. In any case, it suddenly makes killing the rottweiler feel unforgivable. She continues blotting at the scratches, until after a few minutes she guides the animal to the back door. Shoulders low, as if she suspects she might be being led into a trap, the dog follows Nicole outside into the swirling winds. Across the street, sheets of particle board cover the doors of the Stop'N'Go; in green lettering someone has spray painted *FUCK OFF FLORENCE!* Even the cars on the highway seem to be scurrying away from danger. Nicole removes the slip-on leash and stands back as though waiting for the dog to go sprinting down the street. When she just continues to stand idle as though waiting for instructions, Nicole shouts, "Go on, get out of here!"

The rottweiler takes a couple startled steps backward but still refuses to flee. She watches Nicole with trepidation. Every animal has a story—the fact that they are unable to tell them, Nicole supposes, is something to be grateful for.

"Go on!" she yells again. The dog turns from Nicole and gazes across the parking lot, seeming to weigh the decision of whether to leave. Blowing a sweaty lock of hair out of her face, Nicole clamps her hands on her hips, frustrated. Here she is trying to help the poor dumb mutt, to save her, only you'd think the thing *wants* to be put to sleep. Shouldn't freedom be unmistakable? Finally, she gives the dog a swat on her bony rump, and with the lethal swiftness of a snake, the animal's head whips around, her jaws snapping at Nicole's hand with violent clack, missing it by only a couple inches, her black lips curled back to reveal the yellowed cage of her teeth. Nicole jolts backward, nearly losing her balance. A growl like the sound of a whirring machine on the verge of malfunctioning oozes out of the dog's throat. It's just a warning—she wants Nicole to understand what she is capable of—but she gets the message all the same. So there is something wild in there after all, she thinks as she backs away, hands held up in surrender. Well, of course there is. Don't all creatures have their limits?

Something has shifted between them, something irreversible, Nicole gets this and she suspects that the dog does as well. After a few moments, understanding that she is no longer wanted here, the rottweiler turns and lopes toward the front of the building, her stump of a tail twitching, her overgrown claws clattering on the asphalt. Overhead, the anvil-shaped clouds pulse purple. Tiny droplets stipple the sidewalk. Yet, even despite the winds rocking the trees, there is a brooding stillness about everything, as if the world is bracing itself for some great upheaval. *But concerning that day and hour no one knows.* Nicole, her loose scrubs flapping in the breeze, watches the animal once more pause to investigate the flowerbeds before disappearing out of view, into the dawn of the hurricane, never knowing how close she came to extinction.

Acknowledgements

Many thanks to those folks who helped make these stories work, including Weston Cutter, Ed Falco, Carrie Meadows, Leora Fox, Kyle Trott, Joe Oestreich, Coleman Warner, Brian Druckenmiller, Beth Barber, Wendy Rawlings, David Mason, Sarah Dexter, Hill Powell, and Brian and Kelly Shiplov.

For their support and encouragement, thanks to Linda and Dixie Griffin, Dan Albergotti, Colin Burch, Joshua Cross, Lane Osborne, Ryan Shelly, Officer Vince Daus, Mark Spewak, Brice Harrington, JJ Butts, CoryAnne Harrigan, Aswati Subramanian, Jed Forman, John Pauley, The Coastal Carolina University English Department, the Simpson College English Department, the South Carolina Arts Commission, and the Martha's Vineyard Institute of Creative Writing.

And as always, love and thanks to Alexander Griffin for making it all worthwhile. I love you more than anything.

Jeremy Griffin grew up in Louisiana and received his MFA in Creative Writing from Virginia Tech University. He is the author of two previous short fiction collections, and his work has appeared in a variety of publications. He is an Assistant Professor of English at Simpson College in Iowa.